THE KILLER AND THE CURE

She awoke in a large, crushed velvet chair. The darkened room reeked of musty papers and books. Dust particles danced in a blade of light that squeezed through a missing window shutter.

She started to move and was immediately struck by a sharp stinging in her ears. Her hands tied to the chair, she nudged the top of her shoulder to the side of her face. She froze at what she felt: instead of her earrings, two wires snaked through her multi-pierced lobes and shackled her to the chair.

She yanked and yanked her hands, but her efforts only made the chair bounce and tear at her ears.

All she could do was sit upright, perfectly still, staring ahead at the door.

And wait.

She heard footsteps.

She squinted when bright light streamed in as the door opened. All she could see was a silhouette.

"Hello," the man said. "I'm sorry if you've been inconvenienced, but it's something that has to be done."

NAKED PREY

LARRY KANE

ZEBRA BOOKS
KENSINGTON PUBLISHING CORP.

Author's Note

Although this is a work of fiction, the scientific and investigative techniques portrayed in this book represent true state-of-the-art methods used by the more progressive law enforcement agencies worldwide.

ZEBRA BOOKS

are published by

Kensington Publishing Corp.
475 Park Avenue South
New York, NY 10016

First printing: September, 1991

Printed in the United States of America

Prologue

Why hadn't she listened and obeyed? Then none of this would have happened.

"Help me," he had begged her. All she had to do was read the lines. Play the role. The audience was watching, waiting.

He looked away. "Say it's okay. That it wasn't really that bad. Say it!"

Silence.

"Come on. It's the ending that we need to change. Let's get it over with."

No response.

He looked back down. His tears fell on her breasts and slid down in streaks. She didn't move.

"Too late. She's dead," he heard a soft voice say.

The man stood up slowly, cleared his throat with a cough, straightened his body. Composed himself.

He whispered, tried to convince himself. "It was only a test run. It didn't really count. Only a rehearsal."

Chapter 1

Barnett walked into the squad room just as the small weekend day shift got underway. He went quickly to his desk and didn't say hello to anyone. He wasn't even supposed to be there.

"Hey Barnett, have you done your time?" somebody shouted. A few people laughed.

Barnett ignored them and began picking through his bottom desk drawer. He pushed aside a tissue box, packs of sugar, napkins, a paperback, plastic spoons. "Damn."

He began digging furiously then stared up for a second. "Oh, yeah." He picked up a large dictionary, flipped through the pages and stopped at the panda bookmark.

He was about to leave when he saw a stack of fifteen or twenty "While You Were Out" slips. Barnett fanned them quickly to see who had tried to reach him during the week he was away. He wouldn't return any of the calls until next week, and maybe not even then if things didn't work out between him and the captain. It was a warm, sunny spring Saturday and Barnett planned to take Penny to the National Zoo to see the pandas. While working the suicide of a

Smithsonian employee, he'd browsed through the museum gift shop, bought the panda bookmark, and held it for just such an occasion.

The past week had turned into an unexpected vacation. As far as he was concerned, no crack dealers killed each other over turf. No beasts fired automatic rifles into the cars of rival gangs. No wiseguys dropped concrete blocks from highway overpasses.

Barnett felt a hand on his shoulder. "What's with you?" said Caggiano. "You don't believe in returning messages? I left a dozen on your phone machine. Even put notes in your mailbox."

Caggiano spent most of his days in the back office doing paperwork. These days, with homicides reaching a record in the District of Columbia, he found himself outside more in the last month than in the past five years. He felt a little out of practice.

"I wanted to stake someone out in front of your door, but couldn't spare the body," he said.

"I'm on suspension 'til the fifteenth, or don't you remember?" The hand still gripped his shoulder. Barnett politely shrugged it off. "Just came in to get something."

Barnett stroked his salt-and-pepper beard, a leftover of his days in Vice. He kept it short and well trimmed in contrast to his head of unruly black hair.

"The suspension was your own fault," said Caggiano. He looked around to see if anyone was listening. "You can't go around calling the captain an asshole. Not to his face and not in front of his subordinates."

"He is an asshole. What do you want from me?"

"He wants to make peace. Wants you to come back a week early. I'm not supposed to tell you, but he's willing to drop the whole matter."

"Tell him he's *still* an asshole. I bust my butt for this department, and he can't handle me calling him a name so he freezes me out for two weeks. That's bullshit, Cag." He waved his arm wildly. "You know what? I want the time off. I *need* the time off."

"It'll go on your record," said Caggiano.

Barnett laughed. "That's a weak shot, even for you, Cag."

"Standard procedure answer." Caggiano stood straighter. "Okay, now I've done my bit for the captain. Here's what's going on." He motioned for Barnett to follow him into an interview room. It was white with pegboard walls. A wooden desk stood in the middle, plastic chairs around it. A video camera hung from the ceiling.

"We have a repeater, but didn't know it until a few days ago. That's when we tried to contact you."

Barnett rubbed his palms over his forehead and down to his eyes. "Linkage?"

"Females—battered, strangled, stabbed. The photos are grotesque. What he did to these women . . ." Caggiano put a file folder labeled "HO-88-0327; Decedent: Faison, Denise B." on the table. "See for yourself."

Barnett went through the photos and stopped at one in particular. "Holy—"

"Twenty-two. Female. Bet you can't even tell it's a woman."

Barnett studied the photos, shook his head.

"I got the other jacket in my office, a Marie Reed Brady. Want to see it?"

Barnett nodded.

"We got beaucoup photos," Caggiano continued. "And our boy left something behind you're not going to believe. You can see it in some of the pix.

9

Maybe you didn't know what it was."

"The stuff on the floor, sprinkled around. What is it?"

"At first I thought it was background, but he was telling us something. We weren't listening."

"What is it?"

"The first victim, Faison, was found in the kitchen. The room was clean, no food or crap around except some Cheerios on the floor. The little damned O's were all over the place. Blood soaked."

Barnett sat silent.

"Second killing. Body found in the living room. The TV was on and investigators thought she was having a snack. Cereal was on the floor. Shredded Wheat. No reason for it to be there. Wasn't found in her stomach."

Caggiano held up a thick plastic bag which contained a typed piece of paper, and read: "Yes, this is the kind of killer I am. One of the four types as outlined by the FBI in their oh-so-learned monographs. Do you get it yet?'"

Barnett slid his chair back from the table, closed his eyes, and moved his head slowly from side to side. "Who's seen the letter?"

"Just the captain, me, and Quill."

"Are the scenes secured?"

"Only the second one. Marie Reed Brady."

"Prints?"

"'Course not."

"Anything off the letter?"

"Nothing. Used paper from her house. Says he's going to kill regularly after he starts up again. Once we're 'on track and up to speed,' as he put it."

"Did he say when he'll start?"

Caggiano hesitated. "He said he's waiting for you.

You're a person who would understand what he was doing. What's he mean?"

Barnett didn't answer.

"Quill's the one who put it together. I hadn't even seen the reports until after the second murder. I'm so fucking backed up. By that time, it didn't matter. The next day we got the letter in the mail. That's when we knew we had a repeater who was getting impatient with us."

"A serial killer who actually leaves cereal at the scene," Barnett said.

"It's a classic isn't it?"

"Why are the pandas inside today, Daddy? Don't they like being outdoors?"

Barnett and his daughter watched the pandas through thick Plexiglas. The smiling black-and-white bears sat on their haunches, stripping bamboo leaves off the stalks with their paws, and shoving the greens into their mouths.

Barnett stared, but his mind was on the two murdered women.

"Well, Daddy?" she said.

"What honey?"

"Why aren't they outside? The pandas," she said impatiently.

"Oh. Where they come from it's pretty cold. Their fur is heavy, like your winter coat. So, even though it's nice weather for us, for them it's too hot. The cage is air-conditioned."

The answer satisfied Penny, who continued to watch the female, Ling-Ling. Then she strolled over to watch the male, Hsing-Hsing. The pandas were kept in separate areas connected by a closed doorway. Hsing-Hsing was sleeping with his huge arms draped across his fat stomach. He didn't move a muscle, but Penny kept her eyes glued on him for at least five minutes, shuffling from side to side to take in all the views.

Barnett moved with her, listlessly, through the dark, damp exhibit hall.

He thought about the killer. How did he know about him being off duty? Well, that was pretty easy. All he had to do was call the office, and they would say he was out until the fifteenth. That made sense, but—

"Why can't they play together, Daddy?"

"What?"

"The pandas, Daddy! Why is the door closed?" She pointed.

"That's because they don't want them to have babies except at certain times." Barnett hoped she wouldn't ask for a detailed explanation.

"Did they have babies ever?"

"No. I don't think so." He knelt, stroked Penny's blond braid, and hugged her. He looked into her green eyes. "Let's call Mom and tell her we're on our way home. How's that?"

Penny skipped outside and stopped when the sunlight hit her eyes. She turned around and waited for her father to catch up. Barnett put on his sunglasses, gripped her hand. "Got a surprise for you. You'll see."

The bar on Connecticut Avenue directly across from the zoo had an official name, Oxford Tavern, but everyone just called it the Zoo Bar. In a city of come-and-go fern bars with names like "J.J. O' Restaurant" and "Munchies," this place had been a friendly neighborhood place for years. Bartenders still poured by the eye and snickered when they served wine spritzers and pink drinks.

Still, it was the kind of place parents could take their kids for a hamburger.

Barnett hoisted his daughter onto a stool and sat beside her.

"And what will my favorite niece have today?" said Billy Sloan as he leaned over to peck Penny's cheek. He wiped the bar top with a wet rag and put down two cardboard coasters.

"Cherry Coke with two cherries please, Uncle Billy."

"Okay, kiddo. How ya doing, Mike?"

Barnett looked into Billy's handsome face which showed the same thin nose and light complexion of his sister Carol, Penny's mother. Billy was twenty-nine and tended bar weekends. During the week, he was a Social Services caseworker. The weekend job helped make ends meet. It also helped him meet women.

"Coming along, Billy," Barnett answered. He got up, put a five-dollar bill on the bar. Billy waved it away.

"Draw me a beer. I got to call Carol."

Barnett walked to the rear, reached behind the jukebox and lowered the volume. A young man at a nearby table threw him a dirty look.

Barnett detected a chill in Carol's voice. She told him Caggiano called.

"Did he say what he wanted?" He tried to sound nonchalant.

"Only that he wondered if you read the material yet. He said he's glad you're back at work. What's this about, Mike? I thought you—"

"They asked me to come back."

13

"Why didn't you tell me that when you came home before?"

At the bar, Penny laughed and slapped Billy on the arm.

"Officially I'll be on the job, but I won't be reporting to the office. They'll say I'm still out. It's something I worked out with Caggiano." He paused. "That will give me a week to investigate some cases before—" He cut himself off. "Tell you about it later."

"What about the captain?"

"For the time being, we'll avoid each other."

"I was getting used to having you home for dinner," she said. "And the lunchtime dates, too."

Barnett didn't say anything.

"Where are you now?"

"Visiting Billy. We just came from the pandas," he said. "Penny wanted to know why the door was locked between them."

"Oh?"

"I told her it was because they couldn't find any condoms big enough and they didn't want any baby pandas floating around."

She laughed. "You're a nut."

"We had a good time today," Barnett said. "Tomorrow, I have to work."

"Tomorrow's Sunday."

"I have to go over some reports and I want to see Frank on Monday."

They were both silent.

"We'll talk about it when you get home."

"See you in twenty minutes. I love you."

"I love you, too."

Barnett walked away from the phone, stopped, fished a quarter out of his pocket and dialed Caggiano.

A tired voice answered: "Homicide, Lieutenant Caggiano."

"Cag, Mike. I want to visit the Brady apartment. Is it available?"

"Sealed. I got a key here."

"Send it over tonight, okay?"

"Okay. What else?"

"What makes you think there's a what-else?"

"There's always a what-else with you."

"Well it just so happens there isn't," said Barnett. Actually, there was, but he wouldn't give Caggiano the satisfaction. He wanted a pager so he wouldn't be out of touch while he was still officially out. "I'll be busy all day tomorrow. Call you on Monday."

Barnett hung up and turned up the volume on the jukebox. The young man who protested before looked up and smiled. Barnett saluted him and walked back to the bar.

"We have to go. Mom's expecting us." He glanced at the untouched five and pointed toward the tip snifter.

"Where's my surprise?" Penny said.

"What surprise?"

"Come on, Daddy."

Billy watched as Barnett produced the panda bookmark and danced it along the bar top. Penny's face lit up.

"Thanks, Daddy," she said, as she hugged him.

Chapter 2

Harlan Wolfe, cozy in a U-shaped booth, sipped Dom Perignon in Georgetown's River Club. The maître d' led elegantly dressed couples to their tables then glided back to his post. He glanced down at the podium and ran his pen over the reservation list, as a red-haired women dressed in black caught the corner of his eye. He recognized her immediately. "Ah, Madame Wolfe," he said. "Monsieur Wolfe is here. Follow me, please."

Her round hips swayed deliberately as they curved their way through the tables. Her high derriere sashayed with each step. With a well-timed flick of her hand, she swept her straight red hair over her shoulder where it settled on her thin waist.

The maître d' kept his nose up as they walked. He struggled, as he had many times before with her, to maintain a lofty composure as he watched every eye in their path catch her arrival. Male patrons leered discreetly although several were caught by wives and lovers as they stopped in mid-chew to stare and found they couldn't tear their eyes away.

Harlan Wolfe watched the show and it aroused him.

He rose when she reached the table, put his arm around her and kissed her once on the lips. The maître d' made sure she slid easily into the leather booth before he disappeared.

A waiter filled her flute. "You look beautiful tonight," Wolfe said.

Marybeth Wolfe smiled back. "Thank you, darling. That suit looks wonderful on you. That's the one we got last week at J. Press, isn't it? A perfect choice for today."

Wolfe grinned widely, keeping his mouth tightly closed even though he could barely keep himself from laughing out loud. She always adored his smile. It made him look handsome, she thought, bringing out his strong features, the aquiline nose, brown liquid eyes, and chiseled chin.

"Well, don't keep me in suspense. How did it go today? Did you get it?"

Wolfe ignored her question, producing a gold cigarette case and holding it open.

Okay, she thought, I can play his waiting game. She took a G. A. Georgopulo and placed it between her lips, exaggerating the move, making sure he saw it. A waiter walked over with a cigarette lighter, but Wolfe waved him away meanly, almost slapping him with the back of his hand. He lit her cigarette and his own with a thin platinum lighter.

She exhaled and let the thick smoke curl slowly upward past her eyes and hair as if she had all the time in the world. She purposely strained her breasts against the black satin bodice.

Wolfe breathed in so deeply that almost no smoke came out of his mouth when he exhaled. They watched each other silently until neither could contain it any longer and they laughed at the same time.

"You are now speaking to the new junior partner of Wendell, McGowan and Bell," he said.

"Ooooh. That's terrific." She raised her glass. "To the new partner!"

"To the new partner," he said. "To us!"

"To us," she replied.

"Oh, darling. I'm so happy."

Wolfe's promotion had been expected for some time. Five years of toiling at the venerable M Street law firm, hustling new business, and winning battles on Capitol Hill for corporate clients had finally paid off.

He enjoyed lobbying. He strode through the halls of Congress as if he belonged there, taking politicians to power lunches, cutting last-minute deals with the help of liquor, cocaine, women, and, in the case of several well-respected law makers, teenage boys who didn't mind a leather strap.

Whatever it took. He made up his mind about that long ago. He remembered what it felt like the first time he was near the power brokers, watching how it worked, seeing how it was done. Oh, God, the *power*. He wanted it. He needed it!

It was all so far from the helpless days of his youth.

Now he was one of them. Harlan Wolfe, power broker. "Yes, Senator. I can do that for you, but I have a client who's interested in something. Can we talk?" "Yes, yes, lunch will be fine. I'll make reservations at the Willard for what? say two o'clock—"

A thin effeminate waiter sidled to the table and intruded on Wolfe's fantasy, angering him for an instant. The waiter spoke with an affected French accent. "Will you and Madame be dining this evening?"

"Dining? Yes, we'll be dining." He looked at Marybeth. "Darling. This calls for a celebration." He looked at the waiter. "Have the chef fix us two of his special veal stuffed with spinach. We'd like endive salads as well."

"Very good, sir."

As they ate their salads, Wolfe leaned to the side and whispered into Marybeth's ear: "We have something else to celebrate, you know." He licked her ear with the tip of his tongue.

She giggled and touched his face. "I know," she said gently.

"It's going to be perfect. The game is afoot."

"It's going to be terrific," she said. She ran her fingers across her lips. "I can't wait until I get you home tonight so we can *really* celebrate."

"Why wait?" He moved his hand slowly underneath the table, exploring her thigh with his fingers. His body tingled as he touched the top of her stockings and slipped his hand between her soft skin and the garter belt strap. His hand moved up, guided by the lace strap until he felt wisps of moist hair.

She shook.

"Let's go home now," she whispered, as she unzipped his fly and handled him with exaggerated frisky strokes. "To make up for dinner, we'll have something special for breakfast," she said brightly. She laughed playfully as the edge of the tablecloth bobbed up and down. "How about cereal?" she said.

Chapter 3

A sliver of white light reflected off the Capitol building into Carol and Mike Barnett's kitchen window. They sat facing each other across a brown mahogany table. All that remained of dinner were three cloth napkins, two wine glasses, and some bread crumbs. Moments before, they'd tucked Penny into bed with a one-eyed teddy bear named Felix and a panda bookmark, leaving the bedroom door slightly ajar.

The house was one of a dozen on Eighth Street Northeast that had been rehabbed by urban pioneers who found their investment increase fivefold over the past ten years. In the case of the Barnetts, however, it was not so much a desire to corner the real estate market as a wish to find affordable housing that satisfied the District's residency requirement for Mike's job. For Carol, it held the advantage of a six-block walk to her job as media liaison for Wyoming Senator Al Olson. Like many couples, the Barnetts used their sweat and ingenuity to transform a narrow, neglected brick shell into a showpiece befitting Capitol Hill.

Even after fourteen years of marriage, Barnett still

ogled Carol. Her skin was smooth, her lips full and voluptuous. She recently changed her hair style, permed to a frizz, and when she came home from the hairdresser her husband threw her on the bed, said she looked like one of those nighttime soap opera stars, and boyishly smooched her face until she was drenched.

His body wasn't overly muscular, but his chest and thighs were hard from lifting weights three times a week. His stomach showed sinew, a "knotted groin," Carol called it when they made love. He just turned thirty-eight but enjoyed the body of a man in his late twenties.

She moved the glass to her lips then put it down without drinking. "Let's talk."

Barnett told her about his conversation with Caggiano and why he couldn't go back to work for another week. If he did, the killer might start up again. A week would buy time.

He made it a policy not to shield his wife from his work. Many detectives never told their wives about their jobs, left them behind at the office, and played the macho soldier. Then one day, they would explode or turn to drink or whores, and the wives would invariably say: "But I didn't know what pressures he worked under. Perhaps if I'd known . . ."

Although he didn't bring home the day-to-day urban diseases, Barnett let her in on the big cases or those of particular interest. He found Carol a good sounding board for his theories and ideas because she supplied an outside perspective.

According to the blue sheets, the victims were beaten with fists. Victim one was a female, Denise Brenda Faison, twenty-two years old. Police were called to the apartment by a neighbor whose dog whined and scratched at the girl's door for three days.

Police found the victim lying in the kitchen with cereal spread about. She was nude, her clothes ripped from her body and left in the bathroom. No evidence of sexual assault. One of the mobile crime officers walked away describing her head as "a watermelon that had been run over." The exact cause of death was listed as strangulation although she was stabbed seventeen times. From the splatter patterns on the linoleum floor, technicians determined the stab wounds were administered ante and post mortem. The killer stabbed, strangled, and stabbed some more.

Vacuum sweepings revealed no foreign fibers, and the only hairs found at the scene belonged to the victim. Detectives saw no signs of forced entry.

"How do you think he got in?" she asked.

"I don't know. Either she knew him or he faked his way in. I wish I could take a look around myself."

"Why can't you?"

"The landlord ordered the apartment cleaned. They steamed out the blood from between the spaces in the parquet floor. Then they painted the walls. The detectives didn't tell him *not* to clean it, so the owner did. He didn't want the incident hurting its rental potential. Those were his exact words."

Carol heard the owner in her mind and shivered.

"She was a student at GW. Her family lives in Binghamton, New York. Father works in a dry cleaner, mother works for the state as a secretary."

Although these stories didn't bother Carol the way they had when he first joined the department, she could only take it in small doses. She pictured the girl just lying there, the bruises, the blood . . . She felt herself starting to lose control.

Without a word, she stepped over to a chrome breadbox on top of the refrigerator and extracted two

23

Oreo cookies from a bag, put one in her mouth, and handed one to Barnett.

They sipped their wine. "Oreos and white wine," she said, forcing a smile.

All she wanted was a minute's break. She then told him to continue.

"The second murder, Marie Reed Brady, was almost a carbon copy. This time he sent a note." He recited it from memory, including the part about him. He didn't repeat any other details except for the sprinkled cereal.

"I remember when you told me that joke," she said. "Sick cop humor. This isn't like your other cases, Mike. He mentioned you in the letter. You specifically."

He pressed a finger to Carol's lips, caressed the side of her neck.

"Everything will be fine. Don't worry. Why don't you hit the sack? I'll be along in a minute," he said.

She got up and walked into the bedroom, blotting her eyes with a napkin.

"I'll be in soon," he said.

Barnett sat and looked out the window at the Capitol. He watched the amplified shadows of birds flitter back and forth across the building's white marble wall. *Bastard.*

About a half-hour later, he slipped into bed. He nestled his chest against Carol's back, feeling her heat, and they lay together like two spoons in a drawer.

Barnett slept restlessly.

Chapter 4

Barnett woke at 7 a.m., showered, and had coffee. He let Carol sleep.

It took him a half-hour to reach Lorton prison, a three-thousand acre, ten-building complex in Virginia about twenty miles away.

Barnett had phoned Warden Donald Coleman yesterday and said he'd be coming. Coleman was ready when he arrived.

Coleman didn't work on Sundays, but made a special trip to meet Barnett. He wore a dark blue three-piece suit. His white shirt appeared heavily starched.

"I take it this is an official visit," he said.

"Official," Barnett said. He affected an air of solemnity that he knew would please Coleman.

"Certainly. I'll have the inmate brought in." He relayed orders into his intercom, then sat back in his large leather chair and rocked.

"He'll be here in a minute. Until he gets here, though, I'd like to talk to you, Mike, off the record if you will."

"Yes."

"As a DC police officer you have the right to

request any prisoner for questioning. I've never denied you, have I? I can do that you know."

"You've been very good about it." Barnett knew damn well that Coleman couldn't deny him permission to question a prisoner, but he could make it difficult. Standard procedure called for prisoners to be brought to the DC Jail by officers of the U.S. Attorney's Office. That method could be fast and efficient, or slow and drawn out.

Coleman bent the rules and allowed Barnett to take custody directly at Lorton and bring the prisoner back to DC by himself. It was part of a payback.

When Barnett had worked narcotics, Coleman's teenage son Don, Jr. bought an ounce of pot at an open air market under Barnett's surveillance. Recognizing the boy's name, Barnett whisked him away from the scene, tossed the pot into the Potomac, and drove him home. The incident was never spoken of again.

"What's this make?" Coleman looked at the file over the top of his half-glasses and began counting. "The fourth time?"

Barnett stopped him. "A lot."

"I know you don't abuse your position—"

"I wouldn't do that."

"Yes, and I've never pried, have I?"

Barnett prepared himself; for what, he didn't know.

"And I won't ask you now," Coleman continued. "But Frank is still my responsibility, and I have to tell you that sometimes after you question him he's, well, disturbed. I keep an extra eye on him because . . . He doesn't get special treatment, mind you, but he does get watched carefully."

A voice on the intercom alerted him that Frank had arrived in the outer office.

"Tell him to wait," he said into the box. "Guards report that for several days after seeing you, he doesn't sleep well. The last time I insisted that he visit the psychiatrist. The doctor told me, on the QT of course, that Frank has nightmares about the murder and—"

Barnett started to respond, but Coleman held up his hand. "Let me finish," he said sternly. "I'm satisfied that your reasons to visit are legitimate and that Frank doesn't object. His lawyer even signs off. I've done my duty."

Coleman rocked forward and stopped, staring Barnett in the eye. "What I'm saying is: Be careful. Even though I'm legally protected, if something were to happen to him because of visits during nonvisiting periods, it wouldn't look good for me or this institution." The walls rang with the words. "Do I make myself clear?"

"Very clear," Barnett said.

Coleman licked his lips and rocked his chair backward. "Okay then. We understand each other." He turned to the intercom. "Send Barnett in."

Chapter 5

Barnett peeled the red Crime Scene tape off the door jamb, rolled it between his hands, and slipped the tacky ball in his sport-coat pocket. He unlocked the door and swung it open.

A rush of foul-smelling air hit him, and he took a step backward into the hallway trying to regain his composure. His eyes teared.

Once inside, he stood motionless in the living room. He dealt with the stench of death, as he had done many times before, by centering himself mentally and breathing only snippets of air. Slowly, he increased the amount, deeper and deeper, until he breathed normally.

His mind flashed on the killing of a seventy-nine-year-old woman in Southeast three years ago whose body went undiscovered for a week. The uniformed officers wouldn't enter the room, so Barnett went in first. When the hot, putrid air hit him, he sped into the kitchen, a handkerchief covering his mouth and nose. He found a can of coffee, threw the contents into a frying pan, and turned on the stove, retreating to the hallway until the coffee neutralized the odor. It worked better than smoking a cigar, the standard method Mobile Crime didn't favor anymore because tobacco smoke ruined borderline latent prints.

Black magnetic fingerprint dust covered almost every surface of the woman's house. Blood splatters were congealed on the walls, rug, TV, sofa, and chairs.

Barnett looked down and found himself standing on an outline drawn in chalk.

He snapped on surgical gloves.

The apartment's feminine nature struck him immediately. The sofa had a frilly cover that reached the floor, and needlepoint pictures signed "MRB," for Marie Reed Brady, hung on the walls. A wooden floor rack brimmed with *McCall's, Redbook, Family Circle,* and a few copies of *Time, Newsweek,* and *The Atlantic.*

He added this to the victim's profile: read a lot, kept up with current events.

Barnett scanned the tidy bathroom. A glass jar on top of the toilet tank held little guest soaps in the shape of roses. A box of tampons sat on the floor behind the toilet, and there was one toothbrush in the holder by the sink.

The bedroom yielded nothing in particular, but its soft, homey nature again struck Barnett. Balloon drapes covered the window and below it several wind-up pigs paraded on the radiator cover. Stuffed animals lined the antique dresser top in front of a mirror. A photo in a brightly colored enamel frame showed the girl, her parents—presumably, by the resemblance—a golden retriever. Marie was hugging the dog.

The kitchen shelves were fully stocked. Leftover foods in plastic containers filled the refrigerator. Obviously, she loved to cook. Add it to the list.

For all the damn good it would do.

Marie's killer wouldn't be found by exploring her lifestyle. Any link would be found in evidence left behind, not in whom she knew or where she bought her groceries.

Barnett closed the refrigerator and headed into the living room. He shut the front door.

He sat down amid the smell of death and concentrated on the last few minutes in the life of Marie Reed Brady.

He glances at her from time to time, studies his work, the bloody sofa, the walls. Her mouth is fixed in a crooked smile. He leans over, opens the bottom drawer. It's filled with paper, envelopes, and stamps.

There she is, lying on the floor, life slipping away. Are her eyes still open? Blood is on his hands—no. There was no blood on the letter. *He washes his hands first.* Yes, the towels were bloody. Her blood.

He puts a sheet in the typewriter, rolls the platen. Types. Hunt and peck, hunt and peck. Fingerprints on the keys, space bar? Quill checked. Nothing. The chair, desk. All checked. *Pulls the paper out, folds it*—thirds—*puts it in the envelope. Licks and seals. Rips a stamp from the roll.* Quill checked it, too. Nothing. *Moistens it and*—checked, all checked—*places it on the envelope. Does he look back before he leaves?*

He walks outside, drops the letter in the corner mailbox. It's rained since then. Prints washed away. *Think, think . . . It's there. It's there.*

Chapter 6

The sun beat on Rick Henkel, tall, handsome, dressed in a blue blazer which matched his eyes. He stood in front of Police headquarters staring anxiously at the camera. "Come on already. I'm sweating my ass off."

As if those were the words they were waiting to hear, the two technicians purposely moved more slowly, exaggerating every move as they set up lights and established the IFB level in Henkel's earpiece. Morris tweaked a knob that caused Henkel to cup his ear and yelp.

"Sorry, accident. I think we're all set now, Rick."

Morris and his partner Tobin smiled at each other over the prank. They knew Henkel couldn't see them. He was too busy straightening his tie, his hair, pulling down his blazer in the back so it wouldn't bunch up in the shoulders. All the technicians thought he wore pads but they couldn't prove it. Henkel never took off his jacket and, despite his complaint, he never sweated.

"Five—four—three—two and go!" Morris shouted.

"Police investigators are looking for whomever stabbed and strangled two District women during the past week. Although police will neither confirm nor deny it, sources tell Eyewitness News that investigators believe the murders are the work of one person.

"With me now is DC Police Captain Bertram Wilson. Captain, can you shed some light on what we've been hearing. Is the department indeed looking for a serial killer who struck down two girls in the Dupont Circle area?"

Wilson didn't want to be there, but the chief insisted that someone from the department be represented when Henkel did his stand up. Wilson's orders were explicit: wear your best uniform and say nothing important.

Wilson replied, "We are presently conducting investigations into the killing of two females in the Dupont Circle area. The cases are two of several ongoing homicides in the District of Columbia that the department is pursuing."

"Captain," Henkel said, "we've been told by men in your own department that similar clues were found at each crime scene, leading them to believe the murders were the work of just one man. How do you respond to that?"

"I can't comment on specific crime-scene evidence while an investigation is underway."

"If it's indeed true that similar evidence was found at each site, wouldn't that indicate that we have a serial killer?"

Wilson lost his composure. Blood vessels in his nose filled red. "I'd like to talk to the people who told you that. Maybe they know more than I do," he said sarcastically.

Henkel ignored the comment. "Captain, in light of all this, isn't it *possible* that this was the work of one person and that he could kill again?"

34

"Anything's possible, Mr. Henkel. It's a big world."

Henkel took a step to his left leaving the captain standing alone just barely off camera. Wilson felt awkward and didn't know how to respond except to sort of slink away a few more steps. He didn't know whether to leave or stay in the area until Morris stepped around and said, "Thanks, appreciate it."

"So there you have it," said Henkel, looking sternly into the camera. "It's possible, according to Homicide Captain Wilson, that the District is being stalked by a serial killer who has killed two young women and could kill again before he's caught. We'll be following this story, giving you details as they develop. Renee, Tom, back to you."

"Aaaaand, clear," Tobin said.

Henkel let his head fold to his chest and his hand with the microphone fall to his thigh exhaustedly, like he had just run a marathon.

As Morris and Tobin removed the gear, Henkel saw Wilson work a handkerchief across his forehead. The person on the phone must have been right, Henkel thought. The call had taken him by surprise and he wished now that he had paid more attention to the voice. *Call again. Please call again.*

He went to the back door of the van, stuck his head inside amid the monitors, cables, battery packs, and tape machines. "How was I? I mean, was it a good take?"

"You were terrific, Rick," said Tobin. "You really stuck it to 'em."

"Oh, yeah," added Morris. "You got Wilson shittin' in his pants about leaks in the department. Say, just out of curiosity, did a cop really give you all that or were you just blowin' smoke?"

35

"I never reveal my sources, but I'll tell you one thing. This is the biggest story in years, and no one's got the source that I got. I'm gonna ride it for all it's worth. Right to the damn network."

Tobin and Morris sat in the front seat waiting for Henkel to pull his car away. The dispatcher told them to meet another reporter at the State Department. In response, Tobin wheeled the van west on Indiana Avenue.

"What a schmuck," he said.

"Hard to find a bigger one," replied Morris.

Chapter 7

The Winnebago camper, seeping dark exhaust and listing to the right, waddled along in the slow lane of the Washington Beltway. Its driver and passengers were content to do just fifty miles per hour while BMWs, Saabs, and other thoroughbreds in the far left refused to let their speedometers clock under seventy.

The driver, William Wilder, Willy the Wheel to his passengers, perched comfortably in the captain's chair, cruise control on, scanning passing cars for women with hiked skirts and great thighs. Willy wasn't in a hurry because he wasn't going anywhere, just tooling around the eighty-seven miles of the outer loop picking up and dropping off passengers at specified exits just as he had done almost every weekday for sixteen years.

Barnett pulled up behind Willy at the American Legion Bridge, catching his eye with a blink of lights in the side mirror. Another player, Willy thought, as he turned on his CB radio. "Breaker, breaker, you got that Aces and Eights, how 'bout it?"

"Yeah, and you got that Smokey," said Barnett. Willy didn't respond.

"C'mon, Willy, I know you hear me. It's Mike Barnett."

"Don't scare me like that. You know my ticker's still on the mend." Willy underwent triple bypass surgery two years ago. Whatever costs weren't picked up by insurance were covered by his coterie of loyal riders. It wasn't clear how much money came from compassion, friendship, or the basic need for Washington's only reliable and rolling poker game.

"I'm looking for Quill," said Barnett into the microphone.

Willy spotted Quill's distinctive lucky visor in the rearview mirror. Quill had worn it religiously since dealt a royal flush during a game seven months ago. It wasn't a coincidence that he requested Tuesdays off. Light traffic on Tuesday. Less stop-and-go, smoother ride, better concentration, Quill believed.

"He's here, but he's busy."

"Tell him I need to see him."

"No can do, Mike. Privacy is what I'm selling. You know that. Away from wives, girlfriends, and work." He said it like a corporate slogan.

"Now, Willy!"

"Shit," he muttered to himself, then, "Joe," he called to the table. Nobody looked up. "Joe!"

Quiet Joe Quill heard his name but ignored it, more interested in working his way to the pot with three queens and a guarded smile. Even with the smile, he couldn't beat Chuck Cagney's three kings.

"What does it fuckin' take?" he said as he threw down his cards, stood, and walked to the front swearing. "Did you call me?"

"There," he said, pointing to Barnett, who was keeping pace next to the camper now.

Quill grabbed the microphone. "It's my day off, Barnett. What do you want?"

"I want to see your lovely face in person as soon as possible. Where's your car?"

"Up your ass, Barnett."

"No wonder I've been having trouble sitting."

"I mean it, Barnett. This better be important."

Despite his tone, it didn't take much for Barnett to wrench Quill from the mobile casino. Quill's visor seemed to be losing its value, and he was ready to cut his losses. He played two rounds already—two trips around the beltway.

"You owe me big for this, Barnett," he screamed into the CB rig.

Quiet Joe Quill didn't get his nickname because of his voice. He got the moniker because he kept confidences better than anyone in the department. His specialty was "private" lab jobs and although his favorite drink was Chivas, he hadn't had to buy a bottle in years.

Barnett was waiting for him at the Route 123 exit.

"So what the hell do you want from me?" Quill asked, after Barnett filled him in. "I went over that room three times, didn't find shit."

"I got a hunch. Let's go. I'll drive, take you back to your car later."

On the way downtown, Quill thought a change might do him good: from Chivas to single-blend MacCallans.

Caggiano met them in the laboratory. He was carrying a plastic evidence bag from the Brady woman's apartment.

"Wilson was on TV," he said. "Did you see him?"

Neither man said they had.

"He was talking to that blowjob Henkel. Said he knew we had a repeater. Nobody knows about the linkage but me, you two, and Wilson. How do you think he knew?"

"Maybe Wilson told him," said Barnett, "in his sleep."

Quill laughed as he poured himself a cup from the Mr. Coffee by the wall. "Anybody want?" Quill never worried or even thought about departmental jealousies and spats. He felt comfortably out of the loop, safe in his lab. He could laugh all he wanted.

"What exactly did Henkel say?" Barnett asked.

"That a police officer told him the same evidence was left at each site."

"The cereal?"

"He didn't say, but that's the only thing it could be."

"Well, maybe Henkel doesn't really know, Cag. Maybe he was just guessing."

"Could be, but I don't like leaks. I know it didn't come from you or Quill."

"That leaves el Capitán," said Barnett as Caggiano began walking out.

"Keep me posted," Caggiano said. "I got to put out some fires."

Quill put down his mug, snapped on surgical gloves, reached into the evidence bag, and looked at Barnett.

"Okay, hot shot. What's your big hunch?"

"Kill the lights and get the laser," said Barnett.

A few minutes later, Quill and Barnett leaned over the dark lab table. The only light in the room came from a diffused red laser crisscrossing an envelope flap that had been delicately pried open with a razor knife drenched in carbon tetrachloride. Moments before, Quill had seesawed the blade back and forth using measured strokes, a technique learned from a friend at the CIA. The fumes made Barnett cough.

"We don't need much, just twenty nanograms of DNA," said Quill. "That's twenty millionth of a gram," he quickly added.

"I know what a nanogram is. I went to the lectures. Any blood?"

Quill didn't answer as he continued to reposition the laser over the white envelope mailed by the killer. "Still nothing," he said. "Guess he didn't cut himself when he licked it like you thought."

"Wait a minute. Ever gotten a paper cut? You don't always bleed. Sometimes the skin just separates, but the cut is so sharp it just closes up immediately."

"Still hurts like hell."

"Exactly. There's a chance we can find some epithelial cells sliced from his tongue," said Barnett.

Quill did a comic double take. "Where'd you learn about epithelial cells?"

"Told you. Went to the lectures. Keep looking. I'm going to call Cellmark."

When he returned, Quill was sitting at his desk, the envelope now cut in half. He placed one piece in a plastic bag marked "Brady envelope—half" and dated it. The other piece went in a bag marked "For Cellmark," along with several sheets of paper informing their scientists about the sample's condition, case number, and other information.

"They're ready for us," Barnett said, taking his keys from his pocket.

"Going to be expensive," Quill said. "Cag'll be pissed. We don't even know if anything's here."

"Let me worry about Caggiano. We all set?"

"Yup." Quill put the plastic envelope in a Manila envelope and taped it shut. He filled in a form taking responsibility for evidence and signed it.

In the hallway, they bumped into Caggiano.

"Where are you two going?"

"Germantown," said Barnett.

"Who's there?"

"Cellmark."

"Okay, let's hear it."

After a short conversation punctuated by lots of hands going in lots of directions, Quill and Barnett finally escaped into the parking lot.

"Wait a minute," Caggiano screamed after them. "I almost forgot why I came back. Here, Mike," he said as he handed Barnett the pager he requested.

Quill was already at the car and couldn't hear them. "Don't make me look stupid, Mike. This DNA crap is expensive, and I've got to justify each request. It's not exactly kosher to do a partial match."

Barnett searched for a wisecrack, but couldn't find one. "Don't worry." Barnett hesitated. "What did Wilson say about the leak to the TV guy?"

"He said he didn't know where it came from."

"Believe him?" said Barnett.

"I don't know who to believe anymore, Mike. I really don't. Sometimes I get so tired of this bullshit. Just don't fuck up, okay?"

As Barnett got in the car, Quill said: "Didn't think he'd go for it."

"Had to," said Barnett. "It's the only thing we have. Look, Cag even gave me one of these," he said, clipping the pager to his inside jacket pocket. Homicide detectives used pagers for private calls or calls they didn't want coming through the office. Barnett wanted it for both so he wouldn't have to go through the switchboard.

"Have you spoken to Wilson lately?"

"Wilson and I don't talk anymore. We communicate by memos. He writes them and I ignore them."

42

"Must make for scintillating conversation," said Quill as they pulled into traffic.

Cellmark Diagnostics was housed in a sterile brick building in a sterile industrial park behind an even more sterile Holiday Inn.

Chief scientist Jill Huss met them.

Barnett stuck out his hand. "Hi, Jill. Good to see you again. This is Joe Quill from our department."

Jill Huss's lab coat didn't allow for imaginative thoughts about her figure, Quill decided as he shook her hand. Goggles hanging from her neck didn't add to the allure either. That was okay with Huss. She didn't have time for a social life. Under her supervision, Cellmark had grown from a British scientist's invention of a special probe device to a burgeoning multimillion dollar industry based on the most basic chemical structure unique to each person—DNA. The chances of two people having the same DNA was one in thirty million.

Most DNA typing was still being used for paternity suits, but law enforcement was learning its value in homicide and rape cases. Blood, semen, skin, and hair with the follicle still attached contained human cells. Cells contained DNA.

"Nice to meet you, Joe. What did you bring me?"

Under the rules, Barnett couldn't describe the case in detail. If it came to court, Cellmark scientists would only be permitted to testify about what they had done, and not draw conclusions about anything else. The less they knew, the better. Barnett told her that he wanted DNA extracted from the envelope and typed.

As they walked into the lab's anteroom, people

43

hustled in and out, excusing themselves as they hung up lab coats, dropped eyewear in a box, and threw away their gloves.

Each person worked in a separate area on his own project. To keep the chain of evidence intact, the company insisted that one scientist work a case from beginning to end. Huss planned to handle this one herself.

"You know we can't work with saliva. No nucleated cells," she said.

"He knows that already," chimed Quill. "He went to the lectures."

"Private joke," Barnett said to Huss. "I have a feeling there may be epithelial cells from a tongue in the saliva."

"Did you look for blood?"

"I did," said Quill. "Didn't see any, but I did see some caked liquid, probably a mixture of envelope glue and saliva, judging from its opaqueness."

"How old?"

"About a week."

"Storage conditions?"

"Polyethylene bag. No light. Room temperature."

Huss talked as she filled out a receipt. "And you've got the other half of the envelope?"

"Yes."

"Okay, I'll put it in the minigel solution as soon as you leave. I don't know if we have enough material to work with. If not, I may need the other part of the envelope. I'll give you a call in a couple of days either way." Huss put down her pen and looked at Quill. "Okay, let's have the rest."

Quill stood silently, smiling, obviously amused.

"That's all there is," Barnett said sheepishly. "I've been meaning to tell you about that."

"Let me understand this," Huss said. "You're

44

giving me an evidence sample but not a suspect sample to match it to?"

"Yes."

"Do you have authorization to do this?"

"Kind of. Yes. I cleared it with my lieutenant."

"Does he, what's his name—Caggiano, does he pay the bills?"

"It's okay, trust me, Jill. It's a special case. When we find our man, we want to be ready for a match. No deterioration or time wasted."

Huss disappeared into the lab, shaking her head as she went.

"Nice person," Quill said as they left the building. "Smart, too."

As they drove on the Beltway overpass, Quill spotted a Winnebago just like Willy's and let out a long sigh. "Three queens," he muttered.

"What'd you say?" Barnett asked.

"Nothing, nothing. Take me to my car."

Chapter 8

The knock on the door woke Carol from a nap. As she struggled to her feet, she saw Penny bounce into the hallway.

"Ask who it is first."

"It's Mr. Caggiano, Mom," Penny yelled.

"Okay, let him in. Go get Daddy."

Caggiano had known Penny since she was born, a tow-headed bundle. Carol and Barnett had tried for a long time.

"I guess Mike told you about the whole thing," Caggiano said to Carol.

"No secrets here, John. You know Mike's philosophy about cops, wives, and cases."

"I approve, Carol. It wouldn't matter if I didn't. Mike does what he wants most of the time." Caggiano walked to the mantelpiece, studied photos of Mike, Carol, and Penny. He turned back to Carol. "Wish I had done that with Margaret. As it was, I . . ." He shrugged.

Carol knew the story. Before becoming a lieutenant, Caggiano worked the long hours, drank too much, let his job get the best of him. It cost him a loving wife and son. Occupational hazard.

"Have you seen Danny lately? He must be big."

"Twelve. Margaret moved to Phoenix to be near her sister about five years ago. Haven't seen them in more than a year. Danny's supposed to come here for Christmas."

Caggiano always envied how Barnett juggled his life. Once on a stakeout, when they had plenty of time to tell each other about their lives, Barnett confided: "Cag, I'm just a regular guy. I'm not a super-hero cop dropping down on bad guys from skylights, and I'm not a Harry homeowner worried about crabgrass, either. I'm just a man who loves his family *and* his job. I do both well, and I never want to choose between them."

Several years ago, the office bought Barnett a unicycle after a TV producer had wanted to do a series based on Barnett's skills as a homicide investigator. The writing crew watched and studied him for weeks until the producer, Manny Loo, said to Barnett in front of everyone, "Mike. You're terrific at what you do, but there's no sizzle. Don't you have some quirks, some crazy habit that we can play on? Do you cook gourmet meals, drink strange imported beers, build race cars, ride a unicycle? You know, something different." The next day, a gift-wrapped, candy apple red unicycle found its way to Barnett's desk.

Barnett walked into the living room, as Carol was about to respond. She checked herself. "I've got things to do," she said. "I'll see you later, John."

When Carol was out of earshot, Caggiano began. "He knows you're back. Another letter."

Barnett took the note Caggiano held out to him, read it silently: 'Now that you're back earlier than expected, I can begin. Thanks, Detective Barnett.'

"A week, I thought we had a week," Barnett said. "Who told him, damn it! Who told him?!"

"Easy, Mike."

Barnett exploded. "Don't tell me to take it easy, Cag. What the hell is going on here? He knows my movements better than I do. How does he know? Nobody knows but—it's that asshole Wilson. I'm gonna break his head."

"Don't do it, Mike. Wait."

Barnett grabbed his coat. Carol heard the yelling and came in just as Barnett slammed the door.

"I'm sorry, Carol," was all Caggiano could manage, as he chased after Barnett.

Chapter 9

Barnett's growing disdain for the department was starting to show more and more. He wondered lately if he hadn't made a big mistake fifteen years previously when he turned down a job with the FBI. After his graduation from George Washington University on a full scholarship, the FBI had offered him a job in what was the forerunner of the behavioral sciences unit. His major in criminology and minor in psychology impressed the recruiters. But after interviewing with men who looked more like stock brokers than police officers, he chose the District police.

Truth be told, he joined Metro Police mainly because he was a homeboy, raised in Southeast just off Good Hope Road. At the time, DC enjoyed a reputation as one of the best-run agencies in the country. Unfortunately, things were different now.

When Barnett joined Homicide, the squad room had two filing cabinet sections, one for closed cases and one for open cases. The open files got to be so large compared to the closed files that the captain decided to merge the two files for reasons of morale. Now, all homicides—open and closed—occupied

51

one filing area.

The affluent Maryland and Virginia suburbs continually siphoned off the best detectives with higher pay, better benefits, and less chance of getting shot. Homicide suffered most. Once the department's elite, it was now out of the hands of experienced crime fighters and run by administrators and bureaucrats, people like Captain Wilson.

"I've been expecting you, Barnett." Wilson sat behind an oak desk. Almost every inch of wall shouted with shoulder patches from other police departments, citations, and photos of Wilson shaking hands with supposedly famous people. Framed pictures of the mayor and police chief hung behind his head. "Caggiano called and said you were still angry. I threw out the suspension. You got a free vacation. What's your problem?"

Barnett used all his energy just to keep from jumping over the desk and punching his pompous face. "That TV guy knows about our investigation. Not only that, the killer knows I'm back on the job."

"I see."

"That's all you have to say?—'I see?' There's a leak, and I think it's you. I think you let it slip at one of the mayor's luncheons or maybe at the club to one of your jerkoff friends."

"Don't be stupid, Detective." Wilson remained calm and that only infuriated Barnett more. The phone rang, and as Wilson reached, Barnett clamped his hand over it. "We're not done talking."

"I don't have to listen to any of this shit, Barnett." He jerked his arm away. "You're good, you may even be the best we have, but I don't have to take crap from you or any other detective. You're expendable. Don't ever forget that. And another thing," Wilson's voice boomed, "I'm the one catching flak from upstairs.

52

You think I like having the deputy chief ask me about what's on TV? What am I supposed to say? 'Oh, yes, sir, Deputy Chief, I got my best men looking into it,' when all's I got is one hothead snooping around and he ain't got jack shit but I have to use him cause the killer and him are palsy-walsy. 'Yes, sir, Deputy Chief, he even writes him letters. You know the one, sir, the one whose brother is a murderer.'"

Barnett slammed the heels of his hands on the desk and looked Wilson in the eye. "Tell me one thing. Did you tell anyone about the cereal? Did you say we had a repeater? And the sixty-four-thousand-dollar question, *Captain* Wilson, how does the killer know I'm back to work?"

Wilson bared his teeth. "I don't know any of the answers, Detective Barnett, but I don't have to. In case you've forgotten, I'm the captain and you're the detective. This is your case—unless of course you can't handle it. I suggest you look at your own house. That crazy friend of yours, what's his name, Quill? I understand he'll do a lot for a bottle."

Barnett cocked his arm, fist closed.

Wilson stood up, braced.

The door flung open. "Well, I'm glad to see that everyone's getting along like one happy family," said Caggiano. Barnett untensed. Wilson sat down.

"Yes. One happy family," he repeated. "Now that we're all here, it seems a good time to discuss our special case." Although neither would ever admit it, Wilson and Barnett were glad Caggiano interrupted when he did.

"We have a problem, Captain, Detective. Actually several problems. For one thing, our killer knows our moves, at least he knows Barnett's moves. Second, someone's been leaking information to the media." Barnett and Wilson both still seethed.

"I think it's important," said Caggiano with a detached diplomatic air, "that we resolve our internal differences and figure out how the information is getting out."

Caggiano expected one of them to speak but neither did. "And so, er . . . for starters, I'm convinced that nobody in this room spilled." Barnett's eyes shot daggers at Wilson. "I also trust Quill. I've worked with him for years." Wilson returned the look.

"So where does that leave us?" said Barnett.

"Yeah," said Wilson. "Where?"

"It leaves us where we should've been from the start," Caggiano said. "Us against him."

"What do you propose, Caggiano?" said Wilson.

"I propose that we tap Henkel's phone, find out who's been calling him."

"A tap on the media. Jesus, I don't know, John," Wilson said. "You don't even know that's how he gets his information. Maybe he meets the killer in some bar." Wilson tapped a pen on the edge of the desk. "What if we're wrong. Then what? They'll crucify us when they find out."

"What are you afraid of, Captain? Don't like the way you'll sound on tape?" said Barnett.

"Damn you, Barnett. Get out—both of you!"

"You can't let it be, can you, Barnett?" Caggiano said in the hall. "You just can't let it rest."

"No, I can't," he said. "Especially when it's my ass hanging out there, not his."

54

Chapter 10

Barnett approached the sprawling complex and smiled as he always did by the private mailbox on the road leading directly to the prison entrance. The owner had a sense of humor and painted a beautiful sign with gothic letters stating: Prison View Manor.

He nosed his car into the parking lot behind a bus loading visitors for the ride back to the District. An enterprising man who regularly sold cokes and candy bars to riders for the trip was doing a brisk business.

As Barnett made his way inside, he saw a young black woman clutching a baby wrapped in a blanket. The mother couldn't have been older than sixteen or seventeen, wearing jeans, a T-shirt and rubber flip-flops. She glanced up at Barnett as she pressed herself against the wall to let him pass through the narrow corridor. She moved a hand over her baby's head as if Barnett were going to attack. He smiled at her, but she didn't respond. She put her head down, kissed her baby's forehead, and continued out.

Barnett looked around the room which was filled mostly with young black women who were there to visit their husbands, sons, brothers, and lovers.

He offered his service revolver to the overweight officer at the desk who asked to see Barnett's badge before he stowed the piece under the desk. The man looked again at Barnett. "Need a private room?"

Barnett never requested it, but they always asked, and he was grateful. They were grateful for the bottles that found their way to Lorton around Christmas. "Thanks. Appreciate it."

Barnett stood still while the crowd walked around him through the door leading to the visitors' room. Barnett was led into a counseling room with a table and three chairs. By the time he settled down, a door opened and Frank entered.

Frank was three years older than Mike. They shared the same features: prominent chin, sloping forehead and dark complexion. There was no doubt to anyone that they were brothers.

Close inspection of the left side of Frank's face, however, showed a slight depression: a cheekbone broken during childhood that hadn't healed properly. His hair was mussed and his face was drawn. He was missing the attitude walk he had the last time they were together. He shuffled like he was dragging a fifty-pound ball and chain.

"Howya doing?" Barnett asked cautiously. "Any trouble?"

"No. The white section's still okay. Guards pretty much leave you alone. We don't mess with them; they don't mess with us. Not like the rest of the joint."

Frank lit a cigarette with one that was almost gone. "It's pretty much live and let live. The blacks make believe we don't exist, which is okay with us." He paused. "It works out."

56

Barnett nodded.

"The last two riots they didn't even unlock us," Frank said with a small laugh.

The conversation stopped. The pause was uncomfortable for both of them.

Frank clasped his hands together, elbows on the table as if he were praying. He lightly hit his forehead several times with the edge of his fist. He didn't look up. "Anything?"

"Sorry, Frank. Nothing. How'd you do after I left?"

"Slept mostly. Nobody complained far as I know. Coleman say anything to you?"

"No."

"Guess I did okay then."

"You all right, Frank?"

"Dreams. I've been having this one dream over and over. Every night. I dream that she is alive. We're in bed and she's feeding me peeled grapes. Peeled grapes. She pulls hundred-dollar bills out of her pockets and says, 'Here, Frank. Here's for all the trouble I caused you . . .' Then when I take them she turns into a devil. Her clothes, the room, everything turns red with flames shooting out of everywhere and she laughs, 'Frankie boy, you wanna play you hafta pay,' and she touches me with her fingers and burns me . . . That's when I wake up."

Barnett held his hand. "Take it easy, Frank. It's okay."

"Every night I have this. What does it mean, Mike?" Frank pulled his fingers through his hair.

"I don't know. Dreams are funny. Sometimes they don't mean anything."

"But every night the same thing." Frank's voice cracked.

"Do you want to speak to Dr. Clemsen?"

"We've spoken before. It doesn't do any good."

"What can I do for you, Frank?"

"Get me out of here. Get me out."

Mike held his brother in his arms.

I'm trying Frank. I'm really trying.

Chapter 11

"How did it go?" Wolfe asked.

Marybeth Wolfe didn't answer. She lifted her black woolen sweater over her head and he watched her long hair fall back down into place. She settled into the sofa. With a few tugs she pulled off her boots.

Then she finally acknowledged his question.

"Like a charm. I found exactly what we're looking for. He's perfect. Almost too perfect." She laughed.

"No trouble with the computers?"

"No." She began brushing her hair. Occasionally, a knot would make her wince. "Their system was relatively easy to break in to."

She glanced at the mess of papers on the coffee table. "What have you been doing?"

"Well," he said, "I've been busy clipping stories." He reached under the pile and retrieved some glossy magazines. "And I got us some of these."

Marybeth took the magazines. Several pages fell out on the floor. "Disgusting, gross . . . wonderful."

"Only the best," he said.

She studied the pictures carefully and felt a twitch in her groin. "How do they get women to pose for these pictures?"

"How do you think, *chérie?* Money."

"You forgot love."

"Of course," he said. "Love."

Chapter 12

"Do you like cereal, Mr. Henkel?" The voice on the phone sounded serene, peaceful.

"Who—"

"I think you know who this is."

Henkel became isolated from the rest of the newsroom, oblivious to the noises, the people hustling around him. It was like being in a soundproof box. All he could hear was blood pulsing through his ears and the voice on the phone.

Fear surged through his body, and he could barely hold the phone steady. It wasn't so much the fear of talking to an actual killer, but anxiety over this being the biggest story of his life, the one that could put him over the top.

His mouth, tongue, lips turned to cotton. Finally: "Tell me about the cereal."

"I could make you famous, you know." Henkel perceived the disembodied voice as dreamy, fantasy-like yet in control. Strong.

"Yes . . . yes. We can help each other," Henkel said. "Please, I want to know more about you. I want to know more about the two women. I—"

"Yes, the two women," said the voice on the

phone. "You know they were only used to get the police's attention. You know that, don't you?" The voice changed. It was challenging, almost angry.

"Well . . . of course. I know—"

"It was just to get the attention of that investigator."

Henkel was confused. What was he talking about?

"I'd like to meet you," said Henkel. "Get you on TV. I'll put you in the shadows, disguise your voice."

No response.

Frantically, Henkel screamed, "Hello, hello!"

The voice returned, harsh: "No cameras. That will come later, much, much later."

"Certainly, certainly, whatever you want!" *Don't lose him.*

"Do you know the Titanic Memorial?"

"Of course I do," Henkel lied. He knew very little of the city, beyond the power centers of the Capitol and White House.

"Three o'clock. Come alone."

"How will I know you?"

"I'll know *you.*"

The phone went dead.

Henkel, frozen, still gripping the phone handset, listened to the buzz. When he unclenched his hand the blood returned. *This is it.*

He looked up at the wall clock. Two-thirty. He pulled a book map out of his desk, turned to the index. "Memorials and Monuments."

Chapter 13

Kris Rose tried to ignore the car that stopped in the crosswalk just in front of her. She was in no mood to deal with crude remarks from the bursting hormones of college-aged men. Kris had just turned thirty-six, and the only thing worse than getting bothered in the street was getting bothered by men fifteen years younger than herself.

Kris left her aerobics class still clad in a black Spandex outfit, and the only thing on her mind was microwaving a Lean Cuisine and lazing in a perfumed bath.

She felt her leg muscles burn as she sprinted behind and around the car, going for the curb. Stepping up, she braced for the inevitable verbal assault, but instead heard a female voice: "How do I get to Georgetown?"

Kris turned and saw a woman behind the wheel, a street map spread across the dash.

"Excuse me, please," she called. "Georgetown. I think I'm lost." The woman drew the crinkled map out the window towards Kris. "Can you show me where I am?"

Hefting her Adidas exercise bag and pulling her

bracelets up her arm, Kris studied the map. "Let's see. We're at Logan Circle. Right here. You need to take this street, that's Rhode Island Avenue. Take it into M Street and that will get you into Georgetown."

"Thanks a lot. Say, can I drop you somewhere?"

"No. That's all right, I'm only a few blocks from here."

"Are you sure? I'm late anyway. Another few minutes isn't going to make any difference. If it weren't for you, I'd still be riding around these traffic circles."

Kris looked the car over as if it could tell her whether the woman was an honest ride or not. A Jag. Kris had never ridden in one before. "Sure. Why not?" She opened the car door and stepped in.

"Thanks. Go about two blocks this way. I'm on the corner. Red brick." Kris folded herself in the leather seat.

"Tough day?"

"Yeah. My boss is a major jerk. At five o'clock, he wants me to redo a report that's been sitting on his desk since last week."

"Bosses can be a pain," the woman said. "What sort of work do you do?"

"Project manager for the EPA. Contracts, that sort of thing."

"Your boss. Is he powerful?"

"How do you mean?"

"You know. Is he important, high up in the government?"

"He's a director. That's pretty high up there, if that's what you mean."

"Yes, that's what I mean. Have you ever fucked him?"

The word jolted Kris, made her uncomfortable. It was the abruptness of the segue more than the actual word that disturbed her. Maybe it was this woman's way of girl talk, Kris thought. No big deal. Make a joke. "No. He's not my type."

"What type is that?"

"Married." They both laughed.

"This is it. Drop me here," Kris said.

The woman eased the car to the curb in front of a hydrant. She idled the engine and watched Kris fiddle with the door handle. "Here, let me." The woman slid her arm across the seat, rubbing the tips of Kris's breasts with the back of her hand. Kris flattened herself against the seat. "You have beautiful breasts," the woman said an inch from Kris's face. "The outfit shows off your nipples."

Kris registered wildness in the woman's eyes as a hand from behind yanked her headband down over her mouth and tugged until the back of her head ached from the pressure.

The last thing she remembered was the woman's hair; it was red and smelled like strawberries.

Chapter 14

Damian Crystal picked her wardrobe carefully. Underneath her tailored navy blue business suit, she wore a white blouse, red tie, and no underwear.

She learned that cops shied from arresting hookers in suits for fear they might be hassling some straight trying to hail a cab. Damian also found this mode of dress a fantasy magnet for office workers who spent lifeless days pondering the business women around them.

Damian sauntered along Vermont Avenue, hoping to catch late-working bureaucrats before they thought about their long drive to the suburbs. She looked directly into the line of oncoming cars, stood hipshot, and offered her best friendly pout.

Three high-school boys pulled up in a cream-colored Trans Am, and she leaned in to examine them.

She had been wary of multiple customers since a group of bucks from rural Maryland beat her and stole her money. She had toyed with the idea of sitting by the phone and handling outcalls like her friend Marcie, but that didn't guarantee safety either. Marcie's body, her torso marked with cigarette burns, was found in a dumpster behind a very expensive hotel. Damian made the official identification for police.

Damian preferred middle-class men who just wanted a straight lay. Nothing fancy, no equipment. That's when she decided on the business-suit gimmick. That's not to say that she would turn away a kinked-out trick if the money were right and he didn't leave any scars.

"How much?" the kid in the passenger seat asked. "How many?"

The boy in the back seat yanked down his jeans and waved his engorged penis at Damian. "I only got one," he screamed as the driver kicked the car into gear and took off. An unopened beer can flew out the window, forcing Damian to dodge. She heard them laughing all the way to the next block.

Five years in the life had taught Damian many things. The most important was to let things go.

She retraced her steps back to the curb when she saw him standing against the building.

He had come into her life about the time she hit the streets. Not knowing any better, she thought he was kinky, not asking for sex. As they lay on the bed that first time, she waited for the bomb to drop but it didn't. All he wanted was to hold her and talk. Over the years they became good friends, not so good that she wouldn't charge him—business was business— but she often waited for him, passing up other customers.

Only one time did the relationship scare her. He had fallen asleep, and his wallet shimmied out of his back pocket. She spotted something shiny and flicked it with her finger across the bedspread.

A badge.

Just then he stirred and explained that, yes, he was

a cop, but he hadn't arrested anyone in years. "Besides," he said. "We're not doing anything illegal, are we? We're just talking."

He stepped out of the shadows and gently put his hand on her wrist. "Hello, Damian. Are you free?"

"No," she said, "but I'm cheap." Their usual joke.

As he guided her to his car, a green Jaguar drove past. The street lamp was out, but Damian recorded the image of a woman—not in the life, she was sure—wearing a black aerobics outfit. Good gimmick, she thought, good look. Might be worth a try if this business suit ever loses its magic.

Chapter 15

The police officer put his life jacket under his head like a pillow, opened his top shirt button, and leaned back to take in the sun. With his baseball-cap brim tilted low over mirrored sunglasses, he looked asleep.

Jets ascending overhead from National Airport downriver in full power thrusts spoiled an otherwise tranquil scene.

"I'm looking for Molnar."

"That's me," said the officer, moving nothing but his mouth.

"Barnett, Homicide. We're supposed to go for a ride."

"I was just getting relaxed." A sea gull landed on a piling.

"Sometimes I don't even feel like coming into the office," said Barnett, "but then I realize that the people of DC are counting on me, and well . . . someone's gotta do it."

The officer smiled and tipped his cap. "Welcome aboard. Undo those lines, will ya?"

The unmarked police boat peeled away from the Georgetown pier and skimmed the calm waters past Theodore Roosevelt Island. "Used to be owned by

George Mason; you know of the Mason-Dixon line," Molnar said.

"What was?"

"TR Island. His family had a farm there in the seventeen, eighteen hundreds, but gave it up because of the stagnant water."

Barnett didn't feel like correcting him. The son of the original Mason and owner of the island helped draft the Constitution, but neither was related to the Mason who surveyed the Mason-Dixon line between Maryland and Pennsylvania. Molnar was right about the stagnant water though.

"Every so often we pick up a floater in the backwater by the original bridge to Virginia. There's a strong eddy that collects almost everything in the area and keeps it. Most of the time we just get calls about night parties. We give it to the Grasshoppers. It's their jurisdiction."

As a teenager, the island held great fascination for Barnett and his brother. They would sneak on after dark and play jungle hunter along the dense trails. They got caught only once, after they built a fire and Park Police got a call from a concerned citizen who spied their safari from his Georgetown apartment.

The twenty-foot AquaSport surged past the Watergate complex, Lincoln and Jefferson Memorials.

"Nobody told me where we're going," Molnar shouted over the engine's roar. Water sprayed the windshield.

"Up the channel. Stay on the *Sequoia* side."

"Great boat, that *Sequoia*," said Molnar. "Before Jimmy Carter dumped it we used to escort Nixon and his staff up and down the river all the time. The chef, a guy named Seldon, used to give us food. Shrimp, crabs, anything we wanted."

Molnar let off on the throttle as he rounded Hains

Point and entered the channel. He hugged East Potomac Park, lugging the engine, until he was a half-mile south of the *Sequoia*. That put them directly across from the police and fireboat dock and the connecting promenade that skirted Fort McNair. Few tourists visited this area; only those who lived in the surrounding apartments ever walked there.

Barnett looked at his watch. Three o'clock.

Through binoculars he could make out several people fishing, a couple necking on a bench, and an old lady feeding pigeons.

A young man sat at the base of the monument dedicated to survivors of the Titanic. He played his clarinet, oblivious that a TV reporter on the fast track paced nervously nearby.

"Okay. I've seen what I came here for. Let's go back," Barnett said.

"That's it?" Molnar said.

"That's it. Hand me that HT."

Molnar slipped the portable radio from its holder and handed it to Barnett.

He thought he heard Barnett say something about fishing. Barnett mentioned taking the bait.

Chapter 16

Kris Rose awoke in a large crushed-velvet chair. The darkened room reeked of musty papers and books. Dust particles danced in a blade of light which squeezed through a missing window shutter. It formed a bright jagged square on the facing door.

She started to move and immediately felt a sharp stinging in her ears. Her hands tied to the chair, Kris nudged the top of her shoulder to the side of her face. She froze at what she felt: instead of her earrings, two thick razor wires snaked through her multi-pierced lobes, shackling her to the chair.

Kris tested the restraints carefully, twisting her head as far as she could. She thought about jerking her head loose, cutting her earlobes with one quick thrust. Too painful. The wires were threaded up the lobe where the cartilage was thick. She yanked and yanked her hands, but her efforts only made the chair bounce and tear at her ears even more. Blood dripped down her neck and she cried. She couldn't even relax her head without the wires biting further.

All she could do was sit upright, perfectly still, staring ahead at the square on the door.

And wait.

She heard footsteps. Voices. A man and woman. The red-haired woman in the car?

Kris squinted when bright light streamed in as the door opened. All she could see were two silhouettes.

The figures walked towards her, cutting off the light. Kris's eyes tried to readjust, but couldn't do it fast enough to distinguish their features. In an instant they stood before her, towering, looking down.

"Hello, Kris," the man said. "I'm sorry if we've inconvenienced you, but it's something that has to be done."

His matter-of-fact voice sent shivers through Kris. He didn't sound like a madman but why, why . . . what has to be done?

"I wasn't being coy in the car, Kris," the woman said. "You do have lovely breasts." The smell of strawberries wafted into Kris's nostrils.

Kris was able to lower her eyes enough to see sweat soaking through her top. Kris felt a chill on her chest from the evaporation. She looked up.

"What do you want with me?"

The two looked at each other, then back to Kris.

"It's difficult to explain," the man said. "It's not something that we, or anyone else for that matter, fully understands."

"You see, Kris," the woman said calmly. "It's got nothing really to do with you. It's us, you see. It's well . . . as Harlan said, it's difficult to explain."

Kris's best friend, Nancy, was raped by a man who waited in her apartment. She told Kris how the man was detached, but still totally rational in a way she couldn't understand. It was like he was there, but wasn't there. Kris thought about that night, picking up Nancy at the rape crisis center, taking her home, talking all night. Kris kept repeating: "Nancy, you're a survivor. You should be proud of that."

She stayed with her all week, holding her when the nightmares came, then getting calls in the middle of the night for months afterward until Nancy finally moved to Chicago to help bury her past. Kris wondered if she would end up like her friend. Kris wondered if she would be a survivor.

She decided to keep them talking. That's what they taught in rape prevention class. She used her softest voice. "Maybe I would understand. Maybe if you explained it to me."

"She thinks we're dumb, Marybeth," said Wolfe. "She thinks we're sociopaths she can talk quietly to and persuade to let her go. Next she's going to tell us that she *really* understands and that she *really* cares."

Marybeth waited for Kris to speak.

"But I do care. You seem like nice people. You dress nicely, speak well, you probably have good jobs. You make a lot of money, don't you? You have that Jag. Look at your clothes. That gown, that tuxedo, must have cost a fortune. Is this really something that you want to do?"

"Not bad," said Marybeth. "Not bad at all. If this were the Olympics we could hold up one of those signs. 'Longines nine point five.'"

Wolfe laughed and lightly tweaked Kris's right nipple.

"Harlan!" said Marybeth.

"Sorry, MB. I couldn't resist."

Kris couldn't figure these people at all. What were they? Sadists, psychopaths, rapists? *Are they going to kill me?* Kris began to sob uncontrollably.

"Oh, stop crying, for God's sake," said Wolfe.

"Come on, dear," said Marybeth. "Stop crying. Harlan doesn't like it when women cry. It upsets him." Marybeth patted a freshly laundered handker-

77

chief over Kris's eyes and down to her nose. "Okay, blow."

Kris became a child, blowing her nose on command. It helped to clear her head and regain her composure.

"We're going out for a while, Kris. We'll be back later this evening," said Wolfe. "We won't bother with gags or anything like that. You can scream to your heart's content. No one will hear you. They built these older houses sturdily, didn't they?"

"No, don't . . ."

"Don't what, Kris? Don't go?" said Wolfe. "But you're afraid of us. Why would you want us to stay? Wouldn't it make more sense for us to go?"

"Yes . . . no . . . I mean . . ."

"Harlan, you're confusing her. Don't worry about a thing, Kris. We'll be back before you know it."

"Can you . . . uh . . . can you loosen the wires so I can move my head?"

"You women do what you want," said Wolfe. "I'll be in the car, Marybeth. Don't dawdle." He left the room.

Kris saw an opening. "Is it him? Is he making you do this?" Marybeth ignored the comment and smiled. "Let's see about this wire." She walked to a cabinet under the bookshelf and returned with a screwdriver. She reached behind Kris and studied the setup for a minute. "I guess this will do it." She tugged the wire and put an extra turn on the screw. Kris screamed. "We wouldn't want you leaving us," she said.

Chapter 17

"Good evening, Senator Olson. Glad you could make it."

"Thank you, Harlan. Happy to be here. Sorry Evelyn couldn't attend, but she's a bit under the weather. She sends her regards." Olson's wife was in perfect health. She didn't care for parties, especially those hosted by lobbyists. She preferred to stay home and read. Olson didn't care much for parties either, but it was the cost of staying in office. "And this must be Mrs. Wolfe," he said.

"Marybeth, please, Senator. This is a great honor. Harlan has mentioned your name many times."

"Compliments, I trust."

"Of course, of course," she replied. A waiter carrying hors d'oeuvres glided by and waited for the trio to pick at the tray.

"Senator, I'm wondering if we could talk this week about the nuclear power bill amendments?" Wolfe said.

"I thought we've been all through that, Harlan. My mind's made up. I've gone on record—"

"Excuse me," Marybeth interrupted. "I'm going to powder my nose." The two men watched her walk away.

"The association has completed a new survey, and I'd like to present the findings to you. It's fresh information, I assure you," Wolfe said.

The American Association of Nuclear Plant Operators donated fifty thousand dollars to Olson's last campaign through a political action committee. Unlike other senators, Olson made certain not to accept more than that amount from any one PAC. This way they all thought they owned him yet none of them really did. Olson listened to their arguments then voted the way he wanted. The money did, however, guarantee contributors an audience with him or his staff almost on demand.

"All right. Call my office tomorrow and we'll get you in."

"Thank you, Senator. I think you'll be very interested in what we have to show you." Wolfe didn't know how he would come up with new material based on old research, but he would when the time came. The important thing was that he got another chance to pitch.

As if on cue, Marybeth returned with a waiter in tow. He offered them champagne.

Etiquette stated that Olson could not yet leave the Wolfes. It was always more polite, Olson believed, to leave a group after another person was brought in. He spotted Carol Barnett, his savior. "Carol, come here a minute. There's someone I'd like you to meet."

In the office Carol called him Al, but at formal gatherings, in front of others, she used his title.

"Good evening, Senator."

Olson pecked her on the cheek. "You know Harlan Wolfe from the AANPO, but I don't think you've met his wife, Marybeth Wolfe. Carol Barnett, my media liaison."

As his media liaison, Carol had told him always to

80

mention wives' last names because so many women employed their unmarried surnames. Carol was glad to see the lesson had stuck.

"A pleasure to see you again," Wolfe said.

"Delighted," said Marybeth.

Rarely had Carol seen such an elegant couple. She had known Harlan for about a year, walking in and out of the office, although she didn't deal with him. She'd always wondered if there was a Mrs. Wolfe and what she would look like. She wasn't prepared for such a statuesque individual. The two fit together perfectly, she thought.

"Is your husband here?" said Wolfe. "He's a detective, isn't he?"

"Yes, DC police. He couldn't make it tonight."

"Out catching bad guys, no doubt." Wolfe laughed.

"That's what he does."

"I've done some checking," Wolfe said with a wink, "and I've heard he's the crème de la crème in the homicide division."

"And where'd you hear that?" said Carol.

"You. Remember the time we sat in the hearing room during the makeup of S-454 and half the committee got called away for a vote on something else and we sat there twiddling our thumbs. The senator wasn't involved, so he went back to his office to make calls. We talked for about twenty minutes." Carol recalled the incident, but didn't remember what she told him about Mike.

"What a memory you have. That was, what? six, seven months ago."

"Eight to be precise. In October."

"Sometimes he's just a show-off," said Marybeth.

Wolfe put his arm around Marybeth and pulled

her close. "I'm sorry, dear. We've been neglecting you."

"I can handle it," she said laughing. "Ms. Barnett—"

"Carol."

"Carol. I've always been fascinated with police work. Does your husband ever talk about his cases?"

"Sometimes."

"What sort of things does he tell you?"

"Oh, we just talk about what he did all day. Nothing gory, like on TV, if that's what you mean. He doesn't really give me any details." Carol didn't want anyone but Caggiano knowing that Mike and she discussed cases. It wasn't anybody's business.

"He must be a very intelligent man."

"He's very smart. That's why I married him." She leaned towards Marybeth and whispered, "That's the secret men don't know about women. Keep the hunks, just give us a smart, sweet guy."

Marybeth looked at Wolfe, then back to Carol. "You better believe it." Both women laughed.

"Now it's me who's feeling left out," said Wolfe.

"Come now," said Carol. "We're only having a little female bonding."

"I know when I'm beaten. I'll see you ladies later."

"So, Marybeth, what sort of work do you do?" Carol asked.

"I work at Grumman in Tyson's Corner. I'm a systems analyst in the procurement area."

"Sounds interesting."

"It is. I meet a lot of people, movers and shakers. After all, isn't that what all this is about?" Marybeth waved her hand over the partygoers. "Isn't that what Washington is all about?"

"What is?"

"Power, Carol. It's all about power."

Chapter 18

Paul Travis had been picking up after visitors since the Vietnam Veterans Memorial first opened. Flowers—there had been thousands—books, clothing, guitars, rifles, photos, toys: just about anything had deep significance to someone inscribed on the wall. Travis had long since given up trying to figure it out. Who knew what went on in people's minds during times of grief? So it came as little surprise when he spotted the life-sized rag doll propped against the black granite at the far end.

As he approached the limp figure, its head down, arms out, legs splayed, he realized it wasn't a doll at all, but a young woman. This wasn't new, either. He'd seen wives and girlfriends who'd drunk late-night toasts and couldn't stop. He put down the flowers he collected and poked the girl's arm. "Get up. C'mon, miss. This is a national monument. You can't sleep here. C'mon, miss," he said, lightly slapping the woman's face.

He didn't see the blood until the body flopped on its side.

Or the Mueslix scattered in her lap.

By the time Barnett arrived, U.S. park police were

keeping an angry crowd behind barricades. The mostly out-of-town mob wanted to visit the memorial or know the reason why they couldn't.

Park Police Sergeant Ted Green was in charge. Barnett met Green when they had worked a serial rapist case together. After months of investigation, Green finally cracked it by correlating the park attacks to occult holidays, and deploying decoys on those days. The rapist believed he could glean spiritual enlightenment by assaulting women during holy periods.

"Hello, Ted."

"Hi, Mike."

"What d'ya have?"

"She was found during the regular cleanup around dawn," Green said. "Killed somewhere else and dumped here. Nasty business. Weird cuts on her ears. Caggiano just left, but your man Quill's still working," he said, pointing to a figure hunched over the body. Quill looked up and saw Mike, gave him a nod, and went back to work. Barnett, who trusted Green, filled him in on the case.

"Mike," Quill called. "Come over here." Both men walked to the body.

"It's him," Quill said. "Cereal and everything. We got two indicators that might do us some good," Quill said, pointing to the woman's ears. "At first I thought they were knife wounds, but there are ligature marks. It looks like he wove a wire through the earring holes. Even those farther up the lobe. That's the style these days. More than one earring hole."

Quill turned the woman's head in his hands and her bloated tongue peeked out past blue lips. He presented a bloody smudge on her neck to the men. "I'm pretty sure it's from a thumb."

Barnett stood up. "Good work, Joe."

"Don't say 'good work' yet," Quill said. "Wait 'til you see what I get."

Quill took a plastic box from his case and placed it over the red mark to protect it. He taped it in place. He also wrapped her bruised ears in gauze. "I'll ride with her, make sure nobody touches," said Quill.

Quill supervised the loading of the body into the medical examiner's van while Barnett jotted notes. "Got a name, Ted?"

"Found a driver's license. Kris Rose, age thirty-six. Here's her address." Green ripped a page from his notebook and handed it to Barnett. "I'll send you our photos this afternoon. I hope you get this dude. He is one sick puppy," said Green. "I've got to clean up."

"Thanks, Ted. Take care." Green motioned for several park attendants to finish Travis's rounds. Then he instructed officers to announce that the memorial would be open in a half-hour. The crowd booed the police when they heard how long it would take.

Chapter 19

"What are you talking about?" the voice on the phone said.

"You said the Titanic Memorial. I was there," said Henkel.

Silence. Then: "Mr. Henkel. How many times have we spoken?"

"Say, who is this?"

"How many times have we spoken? Answer me!"

"This is the third. What's going on here. I—"

"Mr. Henkel." The voice paused. "We have been the target of a joke. A joke which I'm afraid is going to cost the perpetrator dearly. We'll see which one of us is the strongest."

Henkel was confused. "You mean you didn't call and tell me to meet you?" said Henkel.

"Hardly."

"Well, how do I know it's . . . you know . . . really you?"

"Ask Detective Barnett about cereal."

Again. The cereal. "Tell me about that."

"My calling card, if you will."

Cereal? Calling card. That must have been the clue left at each scene, Henkel realized. *Cereal?* "Can we meet? Can I tape you for the news?"

"When the time is right, Mr. Henkel. There's something you should know. The Vietnam Veterans Memorial murder. Expect an arrest shortly. Be there when it happens."

"Did you—" The phone went dead. "Hello, hello . . ."

Chapter 20

A park police officer dropped off photos taken at the Vietnam Veteran's Memorial. Barnett was about to telephone Green and thank him for his promptness when Caggiano came up to his desk. "Are these the photos from this morning?" he asked.

Barnett spread them out on his desk. "What is it with this guy, Cag? Obviously he's bright. He knows himself. Other serial killers like Bundy and Gacy didn't think of themselves as sick. This guy knows what's going on in his head. He knows exactly what he's doing and why. He's not a loser living in a basement with a bare bulb and a hot plate. He's walking around the streets like you or me. He may even have a wife and family. I need to go to Rose's apartment so I can work up a profile." Barnett closed the photo folder. "What about the tap?"

"I got you one," said Caggiano, "but Judge Millsap insists on having one of his clerks listen and erase anything on the spot not having to do with the killer."

"What? I never heard of such a thing," said Barnett.

"Me neither. He said the media's First Amendment rights took precedence, but that he couldn't in good conscience reject our pleas either, based on your surveillance of Henkel. It was either this or nothing. I'll assign Kuredjian to handle it."

"Okay. Did you see Quill after he left the memorial?"

"No. I called him to the scene then left. I asked Green to hold the fort 'til you arrived."

"Quill thinks we may have a thumbprint from the girl's neck. If that's the case, I want it sent through AFIS pronto," said Barnett.

"Agreed. By the way, I got a call from Jill Huss at Cellmark wanting to know what she's supposed to do with only half a match. She really called to see if I gave the okay for that procedure."

"And you said . . . ?"

"I said, 'Barnett's a nut, but he's my nut.'"

"Thanks, Cag. I'm heading out to Rose's house now. Want to come?"

"I've got so much shit to do, I—fuck it. Why not?"

Kris Rose lived in a changing neighborhood near Logan Circle. The ground-floor apartment looked out over tree-lined streets. People walked to work and it was close enough to downtown for many to come home for lunch. In the evening, however, these people locked themselves inside, away from the pimps and prostitutes who descended on the area.

Barnett knocked on the door. A short, dark-haired woman holding a curling iron let them in.

"I'm Detective Barnett. This is Lieutenant Caggiano." Barnett held out his badge.

The woman stopped brushing and backed into her apartment. "I can explain everything. Motor Vehicles made a mistake. I painted the car, and they forgot to change the registration. I've been down there three

90

times. When the policeman stopped me, I told him—"

Barnett cut her off. "This isn't about a car," he said. The woman relaxed. "Oh?"

"Does Kris Rose live here?"

"Yes, we're roommates. What's this about?"

"I'm sorry to tell you this, Miss . . ."

"Sette. Ellen."

" . . . Ellen. I'm sorry to tell you this, but Kris was found murdered this morning."

Sette dropped the curling iron. She ran her fingers through her damp hair and stared at Barnett. "Can't be. It can't."

"Did Kris come home last night?" Barnett asked.

"Are you sure? Are you sure it's her?"

"We found her wallet and driver's license. We're sure."

The woman collapsed onto the couch and began crying. "Kris, Kris . . ." Caggiano stepped over to the coffee table and retrieved some tissues, handing them to her. "Thank you," she sobbed. "We were more than roommates. We were friends."

"I know this is tough, Ellen, but please help us," Barnett said. "We wouldn't be asking if it wasn't important."

Caggiano sat down next to Ellen. "Can I get you something?" he said softly.

"No." She rubbed her eyes. "Why, why would someone kill her? Was it a robbery? This neighborhood isn't so great after dark, but Kris was always so careful . . ."

Barnett was tempted to lie and say it was a mugging. He decided not to. "That's what we're trying to find out, Ellen. Did Kris come home last night?"

91

She composed herself and began. "I don't know. Sometimes when she comes home late I don't hear her. I'm a heavy sleeper. Usually, we have breakfast together, but sometimes she leaves early for work and I don't see her in the morning."

"Do you know where she went yesterday after work?"

"She said she was going to aerobics."

"What time does it end?"

"I think . . . Wait." She walked to the refrigerator and removed a Xeroxed sheet held on by a magnetic apple, then handed it to Barnett. "This is where she goes, the Y on Rhode Island Avenue."

Barnett scanned a list of classes and handed it to Caggiano. "May I use your phone?" he said. She pointed to the kitchen wall.

"How did she get to work?" asked Barnett.

"Walked. Kris didn't own a car. She didn't think people in the city should have cars. That was the only thing we argued about." She began crying again.

"Just a few more questions, please."

Ellen looked up.

"Was Kris a trusting sort of person? I mean, would she get into a car with someone she didn't know, or could she be lured into a situation which she couldn't get out of? Do you see what I'm saying?"

"If you're asking whether she was street smart, the answer is yes. She gave people the benefit of a doubt, but she wasn't reckless. She was always on her toes, especially in this neighborhood. Did it, uh, happen around here?"

"We don't know. Her body . . . She was found near the mall."

"She used to go there a lot," said Ellen. "Her brother Greg was killed in Vietnam. She would go to the wall and leave flowers by his name."

Barnett shuddered.

"Does that mean something?"

"Kris was found by the Vietnam Veterans Memorial."

"Oh, God."

"I'm sorry. I'm truly sorry."

Ellen began crying again. Barnett moved in to hold her hand. "Is there someone who can stay with you?"

"Yes, my boyfriend."

"Would you like me to call him for you?"

"No, I'll do it."

Caggiano hung up the phone and walked in from the kitchen. He gave Barnett an okay sign with his fingers.

"We're going now, Ellen. We'll contact her family," said Barnett.

"Let me," she said. "I know her mother. That's all she has. Her dad passed away last year."

Barnett and Caggiano stood in the hallway. "It doesn't get easier does it, Cag?"

"No. What do you think about the brother?"

"Somehow I knew there'd be more to it than just murder. I expected a twist. This guy squeezes and squeezes, and he doesn't stop."

"I think it's called 'let's fuck with the cops' heads.'"

A wave of tiredness swept over Barnett's face. "Did you get anything from the aerobics classes?"

"The instructor said Rose took a seven o'clock class. She remembers seeing her leave around eight wearing her exercise outfit."

"It's so close, she probably walked home," said Barnett. "Let's canvas the area tonight and see if anyone saw her. I'll get Quill to make photos from the driver's license. Can we get a few bodies?"

Caggiano didn't answer, pushing open the front door. They stepped into the street. "Well? Can we get some help?"

"Sure, sure. We can get at least two more for tonight. I'll work, too. I know a few folks in this area."

"Who would you know around here?" said Barnett. "All we got at night are pros and johns. Did you used to work this sector?"

Caggiano hesitated. "Once, a while ago."

Chapter 21

By eleven o'clock the local media had sent reporters to Park Police headquarters in Anacostia for a news conference. The murdered woman would certainly be the lead story for that night's TV news and newspapers tomorrow.

Green stood on a podium. Microphones surrounded his face.

"I'm Sergeant Ted Green of the United States Park Police. As most of you already know, the body of a thirty-six-year-old female, a District resident, was found by park personnel this morning at approximately six o'clock during maintenance rounds at the Vietnam Veterans Memorial. We are withholding her name pending notification of family. Let me state that this is the first time an incident of this type has occurred at any national monument or memorial in the nation's capital or elsewhere. I'll be glad to take your questions."

A reporter for the *Washington Post* asked: "Could you tell us exactly where the body was found?"

Green pointed to a large photo on an easel. "About three-quarters of the way down the wall, just past the vertex." The reporter wrote in his notebook.

"On the walkway?" the reporter said.

Green didn't want to be graphic, but he had no choice. "The body was propped against the wall in a sitting position," he said. All the reporters noted that bit of color.

"Sergeant," a woman shouted, "was she murdered at the memorial?"

"We believe the killing took place somewhere else."

"Was there evidence of sexual assault? Was she fully clothed?"

"We don't have any information about a sexual assault. I can tell you that she was found fully clothed."

"What was the cause of death?" an AP reporter asked.

"Again, we won't know that until the medical examiner completes his report. Preliminary findings show evidence of stab wounds and possible strangulation. Let me emphasize," Green said, "that these are preliminary findings."

After ten minutes, the queries became repetitious, nitpicky, and the crowd became restless. Sensing this, Green said, "If there is nothing further, we'll—"

"One last question." Rick Henkel cleared his throat. "Rick Henkel, Eyewitness News. I understand this murder is connected to two murders of young women that recently occurred in the District. Is this true?"

Green replied, "I have no knowledge of other homicides in the District. You'll have to talk to the DC police."

"Why aren't they here, Sergeant?" Henkel said, purposely sounding combative. "This is their case, isn't it?"

The crowd stirred, turned their attention to Green and Henkel.

"Metro Police asked me to conduct this press conference because the body was found within our jurisdiction and because we conducted the preliminary investigation. We have since turned the case over to DC Homicide as required by law." Green looked around. "Now, if there are no further—"

"I have another question," Henkel said. "Can you tell us if anything unusual was found at the scene?" Henkel couldn't mention the cereal without revealing his tip to other reporters. He was saving this gem for himself, but he wanted to go on record with his colleagues as knowing something they didn't. He also wanted to see if Green would squirm.

Green knew about the cereal, but he didn't show an iota of acknowledgment. "I'm not sure I know what you're asking."

"The question is plain enough," Henkel said in a condescending tone. "Was anything unusual found?"

The knot of reporters stirred, tensed. "Mr. Henkel," Green began, "I would call a brutally murdered woman found at a memorial for war victims rather unusual in itself, wouldn't you?"

The crowd laughed as Green excused himself and stepped away from the podium.

Henkel ran and stopped him. "You know damn well what I meant," he said. "The cereal."

Green looked him in the eye and smiled. "I'm sorry, Mr. Henkel. I don't care for any cereal. I'm about to have my lunch. Excuse me."

Green was out of earshot in an instant, but Henkel cursed him anyway. "Damn you."

A reporter from another station tapped him on the shoulder. "Good question, Henkel. Should I give

Dan Rather your phone number?"

Henkel ignored the sarcasm and called to his crew. "Are you guys playing around or what? We've got more stops to make."

"Can he talk to us like that?" technician Morris said. "We're union."

"Gee, I don't know," said his partner Tobin. "I think the rule only applies to human beings."

Henkel said, "Meet me at police headquarters when you're done here. I'm going to do a stand-up in front. And don't stop for coffee along the way." They watched him get into his car.

"I believe coffee breaks are a whole 'nother matter," Tobin said as he lifted a tripod into the van. "Let's check with the shop steward when we get back this afternoon."

Henkel arrived at police headquarters and went straight to Wilson's office. "My crew and I were just over at Park Police headquarters for a news conference. It was a waste of my time."

Rick Henkel settled into a big leather chair in Wilson's office.

"What can I do for you, Mr. Henkel?" Wilson said.

"Well, for starters, you and Barnett can stop playing games with me. I know about the cereal left at the three murder scenes. Cereal, serial killer, get it?"

Wilson applied a poker face. "And . . . ?"

"And . . . I know that all three murders were the work of the same person. I'm the only one outside the police, and the killer of course, who can prove it."

"Get to the point," Wilson said sharply.

"I can go with the cereal story tonight, but I think I can be persuaded to keep it quiet for the right incentive." Henkel fingered his TV ID badge which hung from a chain around his neck.

"And that incentive would be what?" Wilson asked.

"I know from a very good source that an arrest is imminent. I want to be there when it happens."

Wilson sat back in his chair. "How may I ask do you know that an arrest is imminent?"

"Let's just say a little bird told me. The point is, I'll trade you silence about the cereal for exclusive coverage of the killer's arrest. Advanced notice, cameras, the whole shebang."

"Assuming that an arrest is imminent, and I'm not saying that one is, why should I make this trade? Why should I care whether you tell your viewers about the cereal?"

"Because the city's scared out of its mind as it is. Women are afraid to go out at night. We're not talking about black drug dealers in Southeast knocking each other off over crack. We're talking about middle-class white people in Northwest being brutally murdered by a real nut. If I tell everyone about our 'cereal killer' you'll have every kook and crazoid in Washington throwing Rice Chex at their victims. Every copycat killer will be picking up Wheaties at the Giant Food store. You'll never find your man after that."

"You'd hurt an entire city for a story, Mr. Henkel?"

"It's not a pretty job, but someone's got to do it."

"You're scum."

"Can I quote you on that?" Henkel smiled. "Here's my card," he said, dropping it on the desk as he stood up. "The newscast is at five. Get in touch before then."

As he closed the door, Wilson shouted into his phone, "Find Barnett for me."

Barnett and Caggiano were driving back from Kris Rose's apartment when Barnett's pager went off. The phone number for Communications flashed in the readout screen. Barnett picked up the microphone and Communications patched him to Wilson. "Where are you?" Wilson said.

"About five minutes away, coming home."

"I need to talk to you. Check in immediately with me when you get back please," Wilson said.

"Ten-four." Barnett turned to Caggiano. "Did he sound a little funny to you?"

"He didn't sound like Wilson. He sounded, uh, almost human. He said please."

"Yeah, I know. What do you think he wants?"

"We'll find out soon enough."

Barnett pulled his car into a diagonal space marked "For Police Vehicles Only." They walked into the building. Barnett spotted Henkel waiting outside the door, but didn't say anything. The two had not officially met, and Barnett preferred it that way.

For the first time since the investigation began, the detective sensed fear in Wilson's face. Gone was the bluster and bravado. "We have no choice," said Wilson after he described his meeting with Henkel. "If he goes on tonight with the cereal information, our case falls like a ton of bricks. We lose our edge. Worse, we'll have a panic on our hands."

"What made him say an arrest is imminent?" said Caggiano.

"I don't know. Probably the killer told him. Who else?"

"Yeah, who else?" said Barnett.

"I'm in no mood, Barnett," Wilson said.

"Where are we on the thumbprint?" asked Caggiano.

100

"I'll see." Wilson phoned the lab. An assistant said Quill was on his way to Wilson's office. "He should be here in a minute," Wilson said.

"I'm not crazy about Henkel going on the tube and dropping our prime indicator, but he's lying about a pending arrest. Hell, we don't even know that. Somehow, Henkel must know we have the thumbprint, and he's guessing that we'll jump on it. It sounds too pat. It's a setup."

"I agree," said Caggiano.

"What kind of setup?" said Wilson. "I think Henkel's yanking our chain. He just told us an arrest is expected soon to put pressure on us to invite him along, but he doesn't know."

"Yeah, like he didn't know about the cereal," said Barnett.

"Well, if you hadn't made that stupid phone call—"

"Fuck you," Barnett shouted. "You wouldn't go to bat for a damn tap if I hadn't—"

"Stop!" said Caggiano.

Quill knocked on the door and entered without being invited. He looked around and saw everyone sitting strangely subdued. "I'm sorry. I must be in the wrong room. Is this the morgue or Captain Wilson's office?"

Nobody responded.

Finally, Wilson spoke. "What do you have?"

"AFIS came through. I have a positive match and ID." He handed Wilson an index card which the captain perused, then passed to Caggiano. Caggiano studied it and handed it to Barnett. "Aren't you guys talking to one another?" said Quill. "Whew, tough crowd."

"Are you sure about the match?" said Caggiano.

"Textbook comparison," said Quill.

"I don't like it," said Barnett. "Our man's too

101

smart to leave a clear print around for us. In blood, no less. That's not his style."

"Everyone makes mistakes, Barnett. Everyone," said Wilson. "What do we have on the suspect?"

Quill handed him a file folder. Wilson flipped the pages. "Two priors for assaulting women. Probation on the first, then did five years in Richmond. No contact since he got out. Last known address in Northwest."

"We can get a warrant in less than an hour. Let's get out there and take a look," said Barnett.

"What if he isn't there?" said Wilson. "By the time he gets back it could be too late and Henkel will be on TV."

"I've had it with Henkel and his games!" Barnett exploded. "Let's just do our job and let Henkel do his. If he blows it, he blows it. I'm not going to let him control my life."

"Barnett, you're wrong on this one," said Wilson. "What's the harm in letting him in on the raid? It's done on TV shows all the time. What do we lose?"

"What do we lose?" said Barnett. "I don't think this is our guy. That's what we lose. I think this is some kind of elaborate setup, and we're going to end up looking like idiots. That's what the killer wants. Is that what you want?"

"I don't see it. We got a clean thumbprint. The suspect's got priors for assault. He lives near the victims—"

"I'm telling you," said Barnett. "I don't like it. There's something wrong."

"Cag?" said Wilson.

"I'm with Barnett. It smells too sweet. Why, all of a sudden, does he drop a print? It's inconsistent."

"We're wasting time," said Barnett. "I'm getting a warrant, and I'm heading out. If you call Henkel then you're a bigger schmuck than I thought." He left and slammed the door so hard the wall shook.

"I'm sorry I got the print," said Quill.

"Caggiano, go with him. I want this bastard, and I want him fast," said Wilson. Caggiano left with Quill.

His office now quiet, Wilson picked up the phone, then immediately put it down. He sat for an hour, staring out the window, thinking. He picked up the phone and dialed. "Rick Henkel, please."

Chapter 22

Armed with a search warrant, Barnett and Caggiano drove to the address in Northwest. They radioed for a canine unit with an extra man to meet them a few doors away. "Back of the house," Barnett shouted to the officers.

About a minute later, Barnett's radio came to life. "In the backyard. No movement." Barnett responded: "Ten-four. We're going in."

Barnett and Caggiano, guns drawn, walked softly on the porch of the wood-frame house. Barnett knocked and announced himself. He peered through the window and was startled by a cat sitting on the sill. He knocked again. No answer.

Both men holstered their weapons, lifted the battering ram, and slammed it against the door which gave way easily. Once inside, Caggiano drew his gun, walked briskly to the back door, unlocked it, and let the two officers in. He motioned for the one with the dog to search the house. "You," he said to the other officer, "front door."

The German shepherd strained his leash, sniffing under closet doors, poking behind drapes, and crouching under chairs and sofas. Caggiano searched for a basement door and didn't find any. The dog and his handler scurried up the stairs. They returned a few minutes later. The officer pronounced the house clear, but solemnly added: "You better take a look upstairs."

Barnett and Caggiano walked into the upstairs bedroom. It stank from sweat. Mingled with a worn, green blanket and twisted sheets were magazines depicting sadomasochistic rituals and bondage. Black-and-white photos of teenaged girls, hand-cuffed, bleeding, crying, were piled on a night table next to a vibrator with assorted attachments.

Torn pages of largely endowed women, beckoning, begging, were taped to the walls. Wires, ropes, and chains trussed their bodies as they pleaded their case to the viewer.

Caggiano opened a dresser drawer and found newspaper clippings of the three murders. Someone had underlined the descriptions of the injuries and scratched exclamation points in red ink in the margins. "Mike, take a look at—"

Suddenly, a shadow filled the doorway. Both men spun around.

"Don't do that!" said Caggiano.

"Picture time," Quill said brightly, holding up his camera.

He quickly lost his smile as he looked around. "Holy shit."

Caggiano and Barnett walked out of the room to let Quill take his shots. "So much for a setup, Mike," said Caggiano. They watched quietly as Quill stepped around the room, moving his camera at odd angles so the glossy pictures wouldn't reflect the flash.

A voice on Barnett's walkie-talkie called: "Car coming in the driveway."

"Hold him," Barnett said as he and Caggiano ran downstairs.

"Hey, what's going on here?" the man shouted as he reached the damaged door, the officer behind him.

Barnett and Caggiano confronted him. "Do you live here?" said Barnett.

"Yeah, Karl Douglas. Who are you?"

"Detective Barnett, DC Homicide. We have a warrant to search your residence." Barnett handed him the folded paper.

"What the hell for? What's this all about?" Douglas said. He tossed a small cooler on the couch. He was dressed in jeans, T-shirt, and sneakers.

"Where were you last night, Mr. Douglas?"

"None of your business," Douglas answered.

Just then Quill came downstairs carrying his camera and a plastic trash bag. "Finished," he said to Barnett.

"Finished what?" said Douglas. "What were you doing up there?" He started for the stairs, but Barnett stopped him by putting his hand on his chest.

"Hold on."

"You can't just go into a man's house and—"

"Just relax. Why don't you tell us about your hobby."

"What hobby?"

"The magazines, pictures."

"That's my stuff. You've got no right—"

"We got all the right in the world," Barnett said.

Douglas pulled a red handkerchief from his back pocket and wiped his forehead. "I like looking at pictures, okay? There's no law against it."

"There's a law against assaulting women," said Barnett.

"That was years ago. I'm clean. Check with my probation officer."

"We will," said Barnett. "Why don't we start with where you were last night."

"I told you. None of your damn business."

"We can talk here or downtown," Barnett said.

"I'm not saying spit. I want a lawyer."

Barnett motioned for the officer to handcuff Douglas and take him away. "And read him his rights," Barnett said.

"You're making the biggest mistake of your life," Douglas shouted as he was led away.

Standing together in the living room, Barnett turned to Caggiano. "He may be right." Caggiano started to speak when they heard Douglas yelling outside.

Henkel and his crew were filming the officer putting Douglas into a car. Henkel said to the camera, "You've just seen Karl Douglas arrested in connection with the slayings of three women in the Dupont Circle area. The perpetrator's been dubbed 'the cereal killer,' that's c-e-r-e-a-l, by police because he leaves breakfast cereal at the scene of the crime. Why he does that is still a mystery."

Henkel turned from the camera. "Coming out of the house is chief investigator on the case, Mike Barnett." Henkel ran to him. "Detective Barnett," he said breathlessly, "we understand that Karl Douglas is the prime suspect in the triple homicides. What led you to him?"

Barnett kept his eyes straight ahead and maintained a fast pace. Henkel had trouble keeping up, pulling his cables along. "Douglas has a past record of assault. Can you tell us—" Barnett slammed his car door, almost catching Henkel's arm. Caggiano got in on the passenger side.

"As you can see, police are keeping quiet about this most important development in the murders.

We'll have an update on the six o'clock report. This is Rick Henkel reporting for Eyewitness News."

"Annnnd, clear," said Tobin.

"That was great," said Henkel. "What timing! Let's get down to police headquarters for a stand-up." Henkel put his hand to his ear. A message came in from the studio. "All right, wow!" he broke out.

He faced Tobin and Morris. "The network wants our six o'clock report for the national news. Let's go."

The two technicians didn't share Henkel's enthusiasm. They methodically collected their gear. "What d'ya think about this cereal stuff?" Tobin said to his partner.

"Pretty weird shit," Morris said.

"I remember once reading about a guy who killed a little girl and sprinkled fairy dust on the body because he wanted her to go to never-never land. Like in *Peter Pan*."

"What about the cereal?" asked Morris.

"Don't know. Maybe he wants to send them to Battle Creek, Michigan."

"You're sick, ya know that?" Morris said.

Chapter 23

Barnett and Caggiano drove back to headquarters in silence. Finally, Barnett broke out with a small laugh. "Any other case we'd be slapping each other on the back, buying beers for each other. This is just too easy."

"And what's wrong with easy?" said Caggiano.

"Nothing. Except that I know it's a setup, but I don't know how he did it. It's funny in a weird way, don't you think?"

"Douglas might just be our man. If it smells like shit, feels like shit, and all like that."

"You got the shit part right," said Barnett.

As they approached the building, they saw five news trucks parked haphazardly on the sidewalk, microwave antennas fully telescoped. "That's for us, isn't it?" said Barnett.

"Let's go below," Caggiano said. Barnett pulled into the underground garage and they took the elevator to the third floor. Reporters were waiting outside the squad room, talking with Sergeant Tim Boyle of the public information office.

"Captain Wilson will have a statement in about a half-hour," said Boyle, his voice barely heard above the crowd. "All I can tell you now is that we have a suspect and he is being questioned." The reporters shouted questions at Boyle who deflected them by repeating what he had just said.

They missed Barnett and Caggiano who walked in through a door with a sign that said "BLOCKED," but wasn't.

Inside, Karl Douglas, his lawyer, and Captain Wilson were talking. When they saw Barnett, Wilson motioned for the suspect and his lawyer to move into an interrogation room. "I'll be there in a minute," Barnett said to Caggiano.

Wilson stepped over to Barnett's desk.

"So?"

"So what, Captain?" Barnett said.

"What do you think?"

"I think you made a mistake calling Henkel. Did you see the crowd out there?"

"We got him, didn't we? From what the officer tells me you found at Douglas's house, it's a lock."

"Lock my ass. It's not him."

"How could it not be?"

"Don't know."

"Why do you make life difficult for yourself, Barnett?" asked Wilson as he walked away towards his office.

Barnett ignored the comment and dialed the desk sergeant.

"This is Barnett. Would you send the Douglas prints to Quill? Thanks."

He took a deep breath and walked into the interrogation room.

Douglas sat at the head of the table. Ann Rosen, the Legal Aid lawyer, sat to his left. She was about twenty-five, looking fresh out of law school, dressed in a gray suit and flats. Douglas fidgeted with his

112

nails. Caggiano stood in the corner by a fan.

Barnett took care of the preliminary introductions quickly and was startled when Rosen said, "My client has agreed to cooperate. He will answer any questions you have. There is one condition, however."

"What's that?" said Barnett.

"During some of the time in which I believe you're interested, Mr. Douglas may have been engaged in minor infractions of his parole. He will answer your questions if we have your assurance that these alleged actions will not be communicated to his parole officer."

"Ms. Rosen," Barnett began. "As a police officer it's my duty to report all criminal activities." He paced, looked out the barred window. "On the other hand, it's not unusual for police to overlook simple violations in hopes of uncovering more grievous activities. Am I to understand that these actions—"

"Alleged actions," said Rosen.

". . . alleged actions would be considered misdemeanors or no violation of law if Mr. Douglas were not a parolee?"

"Correct."

Barnett looked at Caggiano, who nodded. "Deal," Barnett said.

Douglas sat smugly, confidently, slouched in his chair. As Barnett studied his face, it became clear to him that Douglas was either a sociopathic liar who felt he could finesse his way around an interrogation, or was actually innocent and had nothing to fear from answering questions.

"Where were you last night, Mr. Douglas, after around eight o'clock?" Barnett asked.

Douglas looked at Rosen then to Barnett. He flexed his left arm muscle which had a tattoo of a snake. "I was playin' cards with some guys I know from the joint. Small stakes, five and ten."

Barnett handed him a pen and a piece of paper and told him to write down the players' names and the location of the game. "They ain't supposed to play with me. It's a violation of their parole, too."

"Don't worry about it, Douglas. Write," Barnett said. The suspect turned to his lawyer for guidance. She nodded.

While he was writing, Quill knocked and came in. He whispered to Barnett, "Douglas's prints taken downstairs match the thumbprint on Rose's neck. I stopped counting at nineteen points." Quill handed Barnett the print cards and left without saying another word.

Douglas slid the paper with the players' names towards Barnett, who glanced at it, then handed it to Caggiano.

"Do the names Denise Brenda Faison and Marie Reed Brady mean anything to you?"

Barnett didn't see any reaction from Douglas. "Nope. Don't know the girls," he said.

"A woman was found dead by the Vietnam Veterans Memorial. On her neck was your thumbprint in blood." He gave Rosen a card with Douglas's just-rolled thumbprint and a photo of the print taken off Kris Rose's neck. "How do you explain this?" he said.

Rosen's eyes widened. "That's enough," she said. "I advise you not to say another word." Douglas turned pale. His hands shook. "I swear, I didn't do it. I didn't touch her. I was playing cards last night!"

"Mr. Douglas," Rosen said forcefully. "Not another word."

"Fingerprints don't just fly around," said Barnett. "You killed her, didn't you!"

114

"No, no—"

"Mr. Douglas!" said Rosen. "Silence! I want this interview terminated immediately, Detective."

While Barnett kept his eyes on Douglas, Caggiano stepped outside and motioned for an officer. "Take him to holding. This is his attorney," he said.

"That fear in his eyes was genuine," said Barnett after the three walked away.

"Yeah. Fear of prison."

"No, fear that he didn't understand what was happening. Like a kid who got blamed for something he didn't do. Damn it, Cag. It still doesn't ring true."

"You're beginning to sound like a stuck record."

"Where's Douglas's file? I need to take another look."

"In Wilson's office."

As they walked between a row of desks, past detectives working the phones, people being interviewed, Rosen suddenly left Douglas and walked back. They stood in the middle of the room.

"My client said he thinks he knows how his thumbprint got on that woman's neck," said Rosen.

"Oh?" said Barnett.

"He'd like to tell you himself."

"Confession?"

"Not exactly."

"Well then, what exactly?"

"It's rather complicated." Rosen cleared her throat and fortified herself. "He sold his fingerprints."

Chapter 24

"You mean to tell me," said Barnett, "that you actually buy fingerprints to put on phony hands?"

"Prostheses, Detective Barnett. We call them prostheses."

Myron Couch, owner of Couch Orthopedics, took Barnett for a tour of the family-owned company in Baltimore. They had been manufacturing prosthetic arms, legs, hands, and feet for about eighty years and were just getting into artificial breasts, he proudly added.

Couch was dressed in a brown suit, with matching vest and trousers that were baggy even on his rotund frame. His shoes squeaked as he walked among the assembly tables where workers, peering through magnifying glasses, delicately wired the lifelike limbs.

"Let me show you something," Couch said. He pointed to a glass cabinet containing various man-made body parts. "We call this our museum. It's all the models we've made since the turn of the century. Here you've got the stump and hook. Pretty disgusting. Then you've got the articulating hook, an improvement. Then the technology stagnated for several decades until after World War II. If you look at this one, our PH-106, around nineteen fifty-two." He pulled it from its shelf. "We made thousands of these for men coming back from Korea. Compared to the hook, it was a great improvement, but it still doesn't look lifelike, does it?"

Barnett held the hand and rubbed it.

"Why not?" the manufacturer asked rhetorically. "The skin is too shiny, the fingers too perfect, no wrinkles, no blemishes." He took the hand from Barnett, returned it to the cabinet, walked a few steps to another cabinet door.

"The sixties and the Vietnam War brought great strides in prosthetic devices. For the first time, doctors could actually do microsurgery, reconnecting nerves and blood vessels with excellent results. Suddenly, there was a need for sophisticated prostheses. The Russians, you know, are way ahead of us in artificial limb technology, but that's another story. Doctors could get fingers to work, thumbs to oppose, but what was still missing was the cosmetics."

With a touch of vanity, Couch retrieved a hand from the cabinet and gave it to Barnett. Barnett was startled.

"I know," said Couch. "The skin is a special polymer that looks and feels almost real, doesn't it?" As Barnett held it, Couch poked it. "The covering is pliable like real skin, but not rubbery. Notice the veins just below the surface, the knuckles." He turned it over. "The webbing by the thumb."

"It's amazing," Barnett said.

"I'm sure you see this coming already, but there was still one thing we didn't have to make it look perfect."

"Fingerprints."

"Yes, and palm prints, too. We found that patients

118

deliberately kept their palms down. When we asked why, they said it was because the palms looked—excuse the expression—phony. That's when we, and I'm saying we, other companies as well, decided to put prints on our devices."

Couch caught Barnett studying his own palm and said, "Imagine it without prints, eh?"

"Why not just make them up?" Barnett asked.

"We tried, but they never looked authentic. As long as we were going through the expense and work, it had better look right. We bought real fingerprints and reproduced them photographically onto the covering. In the long run it turned out cheaper than hiring artists."

"How many sets of fingerprints did you buy?"

"Hundreds. The industry didn't want just one or two prints available and have them reproduced repeatedly for every prosthetic device. We wanted to avoid the kind of problem that you've encountered. The voluntary industry standard is one set of prints for each device."

"Where do you get prints?" Barnett asked. "What kind of people?"

"Depends. Obviously, for children's devices we use children, but for adults we try for elderly people. We are very sensitive about a fingerprint showing up where it shouldn't, and the donor getting in trouble. We have a better chance of an elderly person being cleared if his prints show up in a compromising situation. I'm sorry if this sounds cruel, but there's also a better chance statistically of an elderly donor dying while his or her prints are being used. The down side is that elderly people's fingerprints are often wrought with cuts, cracks, and excessive wrinkle lines."

"Do you keep records of who gets what and from whom?"

"Absolutely!" said Couch. "We're very careful about that. Come into my office."

Couch barely fit his large stomach behind his desk. He settled his hands on a computer keyboard. "What's that name?"

"Karl Douglas."

The screen blinked. "Yes, sir. Here it is. I can give you a printout of all this."

"And who received the prosthesis?"

Couch fiddled with the keys. "I don't have a specific person. We show the Bethesda Naval Hospital as the recipient. I can give you our reference number and you can check with them."

Barnett thanked Couch and turned to leave. "Just out of curiosity. How much do you pay?"

"A hundred-fifty dollars."

As they passed the line of assembly tables again, a shiny object caught Barnett's eye. A wire spool. "Wonder if I could get a piece of that wire?" Barnett asked.

"Uh, sure," said Couch. "If you want. It's special stainless steel wire, made just for us. It's highly flexible and won't break under repetitive motion."

"How much wire is there in an arm?"

"More than you'd think. About two-and-a-half feet. What are you going to do with it?"

"Just a souvenir," Barnett said.

Chapter 25

Before he left Baltimore, Barnett telephoned Caggiano, told him about Couch Orthopedics and Douglas's fingerprints. "It's a good thing you're not here," Caggiano said. "The news guys are in a feeding frenzy."

"Wait 'til they find out we're letting our prime suspect go," Barnett said. "I'm heading over to Bethesda Naval Hospital to find out who received Douglas's fingerprints," Barnett said. "Maybe it will tell us something."

"You sound tired," said Caggiano. "You okay?" Barnett didn't respond. "I spoke to Douglas again. He said he had received a package in the mail recently but didn't think anything of it. Magazines, photos, everything. He thought the latest junk might have been part of a promotion to get him to buy more. Included in that package were the newspaper clippings of the murders."

"Of course," Barnett said without much energy.

"One more thing," Caggiano added. "I got a call from C & P. They're ready to trace."

"Sounds like we're doing all the right things," Barnett said.

Caggiano detected even more weariness in his voice. "We are," he said. "Sure you're okay?"

"Just tired. Very tired."

"Don't worry about canvassing Rose's neighborhood tonight," said Caggiano. "I've got people on it."

"Cag," Barnett said, "is this guy just plain smarter than us? Things wrap up neatly then stop—the thumbprint, the way he manipulated Wilson into calling Henkel, the porno at Douglas's house, the cereal joke. It's like we're puppets and—"

"Mike, if you're going to let him get to you . . . that's what he wants. It's like we said before. He's playing with our heads. Ignore it. Follow the leads. He'll trip up sooner or later."

"You're right, you're right. I know you're right." His voice trailed off. He said good-bye and hung up the phone.

For the first time in his career Barnett had lost his edge of self-assuredness. *This guy knows exactly where we're going to look next. He's not just a murderer, he's a game player.*

Barnett entered Bethesda Naval Hospital, an elegant art deco skyscraper across from the National Institutes of Health. He tried to get his strength up for the interview, but he knew in his heart that anything he learned would be taken away. He knew damn it, that even if he found who received the prosthetic hand, it wouldn't lead anywhere. *A fingerprint, for chrissake!*

Barnett walked into a ground-floor bathroom and washed his face. He looked in the mirror, disgusted at his defeatist attitude. "Just do it," he said to the mirror. "Just do it."

Barnett presented himself to a security guard who directed him to the sixth floor: Physical Therapy and Rehabilitation, headed by Capt. Samuel Blumenthal.

Barnett didn't expect such a firm handshake from someone as thin as Blumenthal. The Navy physician wore thick military-issue black glasses and the requisite shiny patent leather shoes. He asked Barnett to follow him to his office. They passed a large gymnasium filled with patients and therapists.

Blumenthal's office held photos from his tours of duty in Japan, Vietnam, Hawaii, Germany, and Italy.

In a cheery voice, Blumenthal offered coffee and when Barnett declined, he asked, "What can I do for you?"

"I'm investigating the theft of a prosthesis that I believe was shipped here."

"I hope you find the bastard who took it."

The answer surprised Barnett. "You know what I'm talking about?"

"Sure." Blumenthal went to his filing cabinet, pulled out a folder. "About one month ago, a nurse reported that a prosthetic right hand was missing. It had been ordered for a sailor injured in a training exercise."

Barnett confirmed the registration number.

"We notified security and the FBI, but we never heard anything more about it. Our patient was heart-broken. He had worked so hard prepping only to have to wait another six months. These devices are made to order."

"Why would someone steal it?"

"Believe it or not, Detective Barnett, there's an underground market. When I was stationed in Saigon we used to see the black marketeers sell them on the street to civilians who had their arms and legs blown off. They didn't get a proper fit, of course, but it looked better than a stump. Here in the States kids steal them for fun and out of meanness. When they get bored, they sell them to amputees. Let me show you something."

Blumenthal produced a folder of newspaper clippings. "Isn't it amazing?" The stories Barnett saw were about burglaries where artificial legs or arms were stolen.

"Every couple of months you see a story like that. I keep the clippings because, well, it's my business. Just out of curiosity, what's so special about this one?"

Barnett told him about a thumbprint showing up at a crime scene and it being traced to a fingerprint donor paid by Couch Orthopedics.

"Doesn't surprise me a bit that some burglar figured that one out," said Blumenthal. "It seems to make sense," he continued, "but, then again, why would he want to throw you a curve if he's just a two-bit burglar? I thought these guys just wanted in and out. No muss, no fuss."

"Some people have a warped sense of humor," Barnett said.

"Hey, wait. Barnett, eh? You're working on the serial murder case, aren't you? I saw it on TV. That's what this is about, isn't it?"

Barnett shook his head.

Blumenthal smiled, looked at his watch. "It's almost six. I have an appointment. Stay here and read. If you need anything copied, my secretary will help you."

Barnett read through the folder which contained five pages. The only item of interest was the name of the FBI agent who made the initial contact. Barnett jotted it down and left the office.

124

When he stepped outside a cool breeze washed over him. He realized he had been going nonstop since dawn and hadn't eaten all day. Wearily, he stepped into his car and headed toward the District. One more stop before home.

The tourists had already gone back into their buses, RVs, and station wagons. Those left were mainly relatives, family, and friends who lived nearby, part of a regular contingent who visited the memorial during evening hours for quiet reflection.

Barnett walked to the spot where Kris Rose had lain. The sun was about to set, casting gentle shadows, and for an instant he thought he saw her body.

He looked at the names on the wall and found Kris's brother Greg. He thought about his own brother and when he came home from Vietnam.

It was sixteen years ago when they stood in their aunt's kitchen after returning from Dad's funeral. Frank held a glass filled with bourbon. Barnett sipped beer from a bottle.

"There's something I never told you, Mikey. It's something I didn't even know until I was over there. We were on patrol and entered a friendly village. It was light duty and we were looking for a place to hide out and get high.

"I'm walking with this guy named Berg, a real character. He kept saying, 'Jewish guys don't belong in the infantry. What am I doing here?' He used to say that all the time, and we'd all be laughing. So we're in this village, and we see this man screaming at a kid. We figured it was his son. Berg joked that he probably took the water buffalo out for a spin to see

his girlfriend, and the old man got pissed. Who cared? We kept on walking.

"All of a sudden, we hear this loud crack. We hit the dirt and look up to see this old guy smiling ear to ear at us. The boy's on the ground. The man raises a bamboo cane above his head ready to whip him some more, and the boy's screaming. We look at each other. We don't know what to do.

"The boy yells for his mama and—now I don't remember the rest happening, Berg told me afterwards that I did this—I grab the father by his neck, throw him against the hut, and threaten to shoot him. He backs down immediately and pleads with me not to hurt him. The boy gets up and everything's cool, but I go berserk. I hit the man so hard in the head with my rifle butt that his left eye comes out, hanging by blood vessels, but I keep on hitting him. Berg said I grabbed the eye and pulled until it came off in my hand. It took three men to get me off. I didn't remember a thing. They said he survived.

"They outprocessed me early, my cycle was just about up anyway, and they sent me to a Honolulu hospital where I saw a shrink.

"The shrink hypnotized me, said I was a good subject. After two or three sessions he tells me that my behavior in the village wasn't related to the war. Maybe it was a small factor; war dehumanizes everyone, he said, but I saw very little action. He said it was all related to Dad beating me."

"What?"

"When I was about three or four, you were just born, Dad was going through a rough time. I'm not sure exactly why, but he'd come home at night and without saying a word he would beat me. It went on for a year.

"Mom used to stop him, but then he began hitting

126

her. Finally, she called the cops. At the hearing, she agreed not to press charges if the judge ordered Dad to get treatment.

"I guess it took because he never hit me again, but I blocked out that whole period in my life."

"Whew. Frank, I never knew—"

"No, you couldn't. You were too young."

The memories lingered in Barnett's head. He rubbed his hand across the granite wall of names and cried.

Chapter 26

Barnett sat at the kitchen table waiting for the coffee maker to drip. His eyes were blurry but not so bad that he couldn't make out the *Washington Post* headline: "CEREAL KILLER SUSPECT RE-LEASED." He rubbed his eyes and focused on the story.

In a highly unusual action, District police yesterday arrested then quickly released their prime suspect in three brutal slayings of women in the Dupont Circle area.

Officials said that Karl Douglas, 42, was a "strong" suspect in the so-called "cereal killer" murders, until police discovered an error in fingerprint identification.

According to Homicide Captain Bertram Wilson, Douglas—twice convicted of previous assaults on women—was arrested based on fingerprints found yestersay at the Vietnam Veterans Memorial, the scene of the latest killing. The body of Kris Rose, 36, was discovered propped against the wall by a maintenance worker during routine morning rounds.

Wilson declined to elaborate on the nature of the fingerprint error but said: "There was a factor out of our control."

129

Police sources have dubbed the slayer the "cereal killer" because he reportedly leaves breakfast cereal at the murder sites. "We don't know why he does it," said Wilson, "but he's obviously a very disturbed man."

The article jumped to pages four and five and included pictures of the three women and a map of where their bodies were found.

Carol interrupted his reading. "Feeling better?" she said as she kissed him.

"I went to the memorial last night," he said. "I found Kris Rose's brother's name. It made me think about Frank."

Carol poured coffee and placed bread in the toaster. She sat down next to Barnett and held his hand. "Mike, you're always caught between your personal and professional life. You claim they're separate, but I know you better than that. I think you're taking this personally and you shouldn't."

"But he named me in his letters."

"It's not personal. He doesn't even know you."

"That's what Caggiano said."

"Great minds, etcetera, etcetera."

"He's so damn clever. Everything fits so well, so perfectly—"

"Nobody's perfect. Not even him."

"He's making us look stupid."

"Is that what's really bothering you?"

"Maybe," Barnett said.

"Maybe he is making the department—and you—look stupid, but are you going to let him dictate what you think of yourself?"

"Ever since you took that assertiveness training course—"

"Don't change the subject," Carol said. "This guy is controlling the situation and you're not. I don't

130

have to tell you that cops are obsessive about control. If they aren't in control they feel inferior. All cops are like that."

"Including me."

"Including you."

Barnett's desk was filled with telephone messages from almost every reporter in the city, from national news magazines, and from major newspapers around the country. There was even a call from *True Detective* magazine. His first thought was to throw them on Wilson's desk, let him handle it. Instead, he called Boyle in Public Information who told Barnett he now had official permission to do any interviews he wished.

"What does that mean, Tim?"

"Between you and me, Mike, it means that Wilson wants you to deal with the media from now on."

"Sure, after he fucked it up."

"I'll take the flak if you want; that's what I get paid for. Just let me know what you want to do."

"If I had something to say publicly I would, but I got nothing."

"Let me make a suggestion," said Boyle. "Wait until you need something the public can help you with, like a composite or description that you want to publicize, then I'll get you on TV and in the papers. Until then, I'll run interference. Direct everyone to me. Say it's official policy that you can't discuss the case."

"Okay."

"The only thing is that you have to keep me posted so I can answer questions. I can't lie."

Barnett thanked him and walked to Quill's office. He was greeted with a big hello. "What a pisser with that thumbprint, eh? Who would have thought people actually bought fingerprints?"

"I know at least one person who knew about it," Barnett said. He produced the piece of wire that he took from Couch's shop, handed it to Quill who studied it, lifted it to the light, watched the reflection. "Is there any way you can check if this wire and the wire that went through Rose's ears are the same?"

"Where'd you get it?"

"Couch. He uses it in artificial limbs. He said it's a stainless steel alloy, high strength, doesn't break under constant flexing."

"We can do an electron microscope scan on particles around the girl's lobes and compare it to this. I'll have to send it out. It'll be expensive. What if it does match, Mike? What will that tell us?"

"It may explain why Rose couldn't break free. It may tell us—I don't know, Quill, just do it, okay?" Barnett said sharply.

Quill looked at Barnett, hurt, and didn't say anything.

"I'm sorry. It's not your fault," Barnett said.

"I'll take care of it and let you know," Quill said coldly.

Barnett wanted to apologize again, but Quill had already walked away. He felt awful.

At his desk, Barnett closed his eyes, then twitched as if someone had woken him from a deep sleep. He shook his head to focus his thoughts.

Barnett dialed the FBI agent listed on the hospital's burglary report. Special Agent Vincent Turpin answered, and they exchanged chitchat about mutual friends in both departments until Turpin established that Barnett was okay. Despite public perception, the FBI and local police didn't get along. Jealousy existed and neither traded information except to personal contacts, friends of friends, or by direct order from the upper echelon.

"Don't have much to tell you, Detective Barnett. Off the record, we didn't take it very seriously. The only piece of information we have is from an orderly who came into work around three in the morning. He saw a woman in the parking lot carrying a package with the same kind of wrapping that the artificial arm came in. He didn't get a good look at her face but said she had, and I quote, 'a knockout body.' She drove a big car, didn't know what kind. I'm afraid that's it. Nobody else, not the guards nor the rest of the staff, saw anything."

Barnett took the witness's name and phone number, and told Turpin he owed him a drink.

Calling the FBI made Barnett realize what he had to do next. He got his textbooks and work sheets that he used in profiling school, along with the three case files, and sequestered himself in an unused office.

Barnett hadn't worked a profile in several years, and that was for the serial rapist case in which he and Green collaborated. He started to reread his notes but, for an instant, his concentration was shattered by the killer's mocking first letter. *"Yes, I'm one of the four types . . ."*

Intuitively, Barnett thought he knew what the profiling would tell him, but going through the exercise would make certain. He also looked at it as a chance to go over the files and maybe see something that he hadn't seen before. In the back of his mind, he also knew it was a way to rebuild his self-confidence, a way to capture control. Isn't that what Carol had said? He wasn't happy unless he was in control.

Barnett readjusted the light from a gooseneck lamp on the desk and sorted his papers. His notes were sloppy, and he had trouble reading them. He had written so quickly at the time.

"Visionary Type," he said. "Responds to voices or visions. Directed by God or other deity. Out of touch with reality. Psychotic. Rare, possibly biochemical. Can't rest until does bidding of voices. Son of Sam."

The instructor had told the class about the Son of Sam case in New York City in which David Berkowitz killed six people. Berkowitz said that a demon had spoken to him through a neighbor's dog, ordering him to kill. He wouldn't get any peace until he obeyed.

"Mission-oriented type. Get rid of certain kind of person/unworthy groups, i.e., prostitutes, religions, bag ladies. Teach them a lesson." Barnett flashed on the office worker who killed homeless people with poisoned sandwiches thrown in trash barrels in Farragut Square Park.

The third type disturbed Barnett the most because it was the most vicious and senseless. The so-called "hedonistic" type killed for the fun of it. At the time he thought that even though the other types had crazy reasons for their actions, "at least they had reasons," he had written. "Thrillseekers. Derive pleasure from act itself. Excitement. Focus on act. Most common for man/woman teams. Subcategory: Lust murderer—sexual arousal, gratification, sometimes torture, mutilation. Watch media, like attention."

The last type was dubbed the "power or control-oriented" killer. "Derives satisfaction from absolute life or death control over victim. Victims made helpless. Determines victim's fate. Most complicated motives. Hard to analyze. Focus on act same as hedonistic."

Barnett scanned his notes again, noticing how some of the traits overlapped. That didn't bother him the way it did others in his class. They were looking for a neat list of characteristics that would lead directly to the killer despite the instructor's warning that profiling was an art, not a science. Barnett looked at profiling as an edge, nothing more. Identifying the various factors would allow him to decide into which of the four types this killer fit.

Most of the data for the FBI's profiling system came from the VICAP program which relied on local police and FBI agents to fill out lengthy questionnaires about violent offenders. A lot of local agencies refused to fill them out because they didn't feel any benefit from the program. Barnett once saw a sign above a desk: "FBI Motto: Thank you for your help, officer. We can take it from here."

Barnett had participated in several interviews with convicted killers and was amazed how much these people would tell about their crimes. That was part of the problem, Barnett believed. The profiling information was skewed towards those killers that talked the most. Of course, that made sense. The FBI knew the most about those who told them the most.

That's probably why, in Barnett's estimation, the profiling system only rendered a fifty-percent success rate. When it was right, however, it was close to one-hundred percent right in almost every aspect of the profile.

Barnett took a large piece of paper and with a ruler drew a horizontal line across the top on which he wrote TYPE OF KILLER. He turned the ruler vertically, on the left side, and traced a line which formed a column he labeled FACTORS.

Barnett got up to stretch his arms and legs. He walked into the bull pen hoping someone would start a conversation, but no one did. The office was lifeless save two detectives reading quietly at their desks. Everyone else was out on the street.

Barnett walked back into the office. He spent the next two hours studying the case files of the three murdered women and making notes on a yellow legal pad. He worked feverishly. His neck muscles and upper back ached when he finally looked up.

He felt like his head was chock full of disparate chunks of information that craved to be molded into logical form. He turned to his notes, then to his empty chart.

Under the column headed FACTORS he wrote the word *Victims*. He scanned his memory and quickly wrote: "specific." *Of course. He chose them, didn't he?*

He thought about the three victims, their names, in the case of Kris Rose, her brother's name inscribed in the wall. He wrote: "nonrandom." The next entry wasn't so easy. Affiliative or stranger? Barnett didn't have any evidence that the women knew their killer. Then again, could he have known them, even casually? He didn't think so, but the chart had to be absolutely accurate. He penciled in "stranger" with a question mark after it.

Next came *Methods*. Barnett looked at his notes. *He didn't just kill them. No, he tortured them, bound them, taunted them. Killing wasn't the main goal.* He wasn't "act focused," he was "process focused." Barnett made that notation. Planned or spontaneous? He wrote: "planned" and underlined it, put a star next to it.

Organized or disorganized? This was the most argued point in profiling. Yes, it was easy to figure. Man, was this guy organized. Nothing was left astray, but it was the interpretation of that word that was troublesome. Barnett didn't always buy the belief that an organized crime scene meant anything special. Sometimes mistakes happened despite the killer's precise planning, a left weapon, an errant fingerprint. Barnett laughed. *Yeah, errant fingerprint.* Usually organized killers hid their bodies. This killer did just the opposite. He purposely left them in the open. He jotted: "organized" and left it at that.

Before he filled in *Murder Locations*, Barnett thought for a moment. Most serial killers, like Bundy, were geographically dispersed or "unstable" in profiling language. They killed and moved on. His guy was geographically concentrated, but only because he wanted to target a specific spectator. *Me.* He wrote: "concentrated," then made a little asterisk. On the bottom of the sheet he marked a matching asterisk and wrote: "not applicable."

Barnett went to his desk, retrieved a copy of *Serial Murder* by Holmes and De Burger. He turned to their chart with the caption "Homicidal Behavior Patterns: Modal Characteristic by Type of Serial Murderers."

He compared his chart with theirs. The points were exact. Textbook, as the psychologists would say.

Power/Control-Oriented Type.

Barnett was elated, satisfied that he hadn't wasted his time. At least he knew something about the killer that he didn't know before. He was a power/control type, and that meant Barnett could construct a fairly accurate psychological, maybe even a physical, profile.

An edge.

Chapter 27

"Are you free?"

"No, but I'm cheap."

They met in the parlor of the Tabard Inn. He was glad that she dressed conservatively. After several drinks, they decided to get a room upstairs. They had been here before, many times, to savor the tranquillity of the only bed-and-breakfast in the heart of the District. Once inside, the mean streets were a million miles away. "I've been wondering how you've been. I haven't seen you in a while," she said.

"I've been busy with work. This cereal killer case—I've told you about it—is keeping me jumping. I haven't had a moment to think. In fact, I have to get back on the street soon."

"Some of the girls said they noticed plainclothes walking the neighborhood tonight, asking questions about the Rose woman. They working for you?"

"Yes. We think she was kidnapped around Logan Circle. She lived nearby." Caggiano sat in an overstuffed chair. His shoes and shirt were off. Damian lay on the cover of the four-poster bed.

"Is she the one they found by the Vietnam memorial?"

"That's her. I've got a picture." Caggiano held the photo for Damian to see. She took it in her hand. "She was wearing a black Spandex exercise outfit when we found her."

Damian squinted. "Hey, I know her. I mean I've seen her somewhere. I can't remember . . . Wait . . . The last time you and I were together, she was getting into a car. I remember thinking the outfit was . . . well, never mind."

Caggiano stirred, excited. "What'd you see?"

"A green car. I remember that, and I think a woman was driving. I'm not sure about that part. The driver had long hair, but that doesn't mean anything, styles being what they are today."

"Where exactly?" Caggiano asked.

"On the corner. Where I met you. By the Circle, wasn't it?"

"I think so."

"Do you think it really could have been the killer?" Damian leaned back against the pillows, sat upright, and turned to him. Suddenly, it struck her. The green car. Long-haired driver. *No, no, it couldn't be.*

She turned on her sweet whore voice usually reserved for other customers. Manipulative but . . . Whatever it took to get what she wanted. She straightened her stockings, ran her hand over her thigh, smoothed her dress. "John, please stay with me tonight."

"I'm supposed to be canvassing the neighborhood. Talk to your sisters." He smiled.

"Please. Just tonight. Stay with me." Her eyes begged.

He'd never seen this side of her, vulnerable, tender, frightened.

140

Damian watched Caggiano get up, a perplexed look on his face. He walked toward the light switch. She closed her eyes, held her hands out, waited for him to return and lie on top of her.

The darkness covered them. Her mind reeled. *Oh, dear God. Don't let it be them.*

Chapter 28

It was an old Silver Spring neighborhood off Georgia Avenue with a mixture of split-level brick homes, small two stories, and tiny bungalows. Children's plastic toys, bicycles, and muscle cars undergoing polish were scattered over driveways and lawns. One could count on at least one house per block being repaired, painted, or spackled on any given Saturday morning.

Barnett pulled up to a tidy ranch unit with a man pushing a mower around several thin pine trees. He looked at Barnett getting out of his car, cut the engine, and waited.

"I'm looking for Mr. Stanley Guillmond."

The man was wearing cut-off jeans, high white socks topped with red and white stripes, sneakers, and a T-shirt with a bank logo. He sized up Barnett quickly. "You the police or something?"

Barnett took out his badge. "District police. Mike Barnett. You Guillmond?"

He released his grip on the mower handle and relaxed. "That's me. Knew you looked official," he said. "What do you want?"

"I'm investigating the theft of a prosthesis from

Bethesda Naval Hospital. I got your name from the FBI."

"Oh, yeah. You still looking for that arm?"

Barnett didn't answer. "I understand you saw someone leaving the hospital with something that looked like the arm."

"No, no, no, no," he sang. "What I told that FBI fellow was that I saw someone carrying a package and the package was covered with wrapping like the kind they ship the arms in. *That's* what I said."

"How do you know what kind of paper the arms come in?"

"Wrapping," he corrected Barnett. "I've been working at Bethesda for eleven years. Since I got out of the Navy. I know what they look like."

"Tell me what you saw."

"Okay. I was coming in late, about three. My car," he pointed to the driveway at a red Chevy Nova, "wouldn't start right away. Had to jump it from my wife's car. Anyways, I called and said I'd be late. I parked in the lot and was walking inside when I saw this woman." He looked around at the house. "She had a bod . . . I'm telling you. Whew. She was walking out, calm as anything, carrying this package. She gets into a car and drives away. That's it."

"What did she look like? Can you describe her?"

"I told you. She was built. Tall, long hair—"

"What color?"

"Don't know. It was shiny, but I don't know what color."

"Clothes?"

"She wore a dress—tight, real tight. She sashayed her bootie—"

"What color were her clothes?"

"Don't remember, but she had one of those suits

that women wear to look like men. You know, with the matching jacket."

"You said she got into a car."

"It was a big car. I'm pretty sure it was green, but I don't know what type. I mean, I would know it if I remembered, but I really wasn't paying attention. I was in a rush to get to work. I was late as it was. The only reason I paid any attention was because of her looks. Well, that and the fact that it was three in the morning. Usually don't see much of anyone going in or out at that time."

Barnett scribbled in his notebook. "Anything else about the woman?"

Guillmond thought for a moment, put his hand to his lip. "There was one other thing." He looked around again. "I didn't tell the FBI fellow this. I didn't think of it until after I spoke to him, and I wasn't going to call him back."

Barnett moved in closer.

"It's probably not important anyway."

Barnett didn't respond.

"When she got into the car, she put the package in her lap and moved it. You know. Moved it. You know what I mean?" His eyebrows traveled up.

"You mean like . . ."

"Yeah, you know. *Moved* it."

"Didn't you think that was strange?"

"It didn't register. I thought she was adjusting her seat belt or something. It wasn't until later that I realized what was going on."

"Maybe she *was* just fiddling with her seat belt."

Guillmond nodded and smiled. "Maybe. I could be wrong. I've been wrong about things before." He looked at Barnett like they were drinking buddies and whispered, "But I sure think about it a lot."

Chapter 29

Barnett had just locked his front door when the pager on his belt warbled. He checked the number in the screen, stepped back inside, and called Caggiano's home.

"You been out all night?" said Barnett. "I've been trying to reach you."

"Didn't get home until . . . well . . . very early this morning. Wanted to let you know about something soon as I could." He related Damian's story, leaving out his personal relationship with her. It was a part of his life of which he wasn't particularly proud.

"Cag," Barnett said, "from what you're saying, and what the FBI told me, the green car is the connection."

"And a possible female accomplice," said Caggiano.

"That puts a new spin on things. I was on my way to NIMH. If you want to see the preliminary profile workup, it's on my desk."

"Okay," said Caggiano. "You sure sound more upbeat today."

"I've been an asshole lately."

"You sure have. That wife of yours set you straight?"

"Doesn't she always?" Barnett laughed and thought about the expression on Quill's face when he would find the gift-wrapped bottle of MacCallans sitting on his desk.

Even with the door closed, Dr. Monika Sidor's office faintly smelled of the monkeys, shrews, and lemurs that lived in nearby cages. She sat, templing her fingers, piercing Barnett with the lightest blue eyes in the world.

He presented the surroundings with his hands. "You like this better than people, Monny?"

"Less trouble. They don't kill anybody."

"Don't you miss the action?"

"You mean like a razor at my neck for an hour? I need that like I need another head."

Barnett met Monny when she was assigned to MPD as a crisis psychiatrist. They used her to talk down jumpers, negotiate hostage situations, and interrogate particularly loony suspects. She had worked for six months out of headquarters when she was called to a barricade location—a father who held his three children inside a small wooden house threatening to kill them with a homemade bomb. He said he wanted his estranged wife to come back home. Police tried to locate the wife but couldn't.

Over a three-hour period, Monny was making headway with the man, gaining his trust over the phone. Then, against the advice of the lieutenant in charge, she entered the house where the husband immediately pounced on her and held a straight razor to her neck, demanding that police find his wife and bring her to him.

There was no wife. She had died two weeks earlier, caught in the back by a stray bullet from drug dealers OK Corralling it in broad daylight.

Doctors at DC General forced three pints of blood into Monny before she regained consciousness. A day after her discharge, she gave her resignation and took a six-month vacation in St. Thomas. "All I want is a normal job, come home at night, watch TV, munch popcorn. Get it, Barnett?" she had said as she was packing her bags.

When she returned, she took a contract position at the National Institute of Mental Health, finding out why monkeys would rather eat cocaine than food.

"Look at this," she said smiling. "I'm dealing to monkeys and they love me for it. Can you say the same, Barnett?"

"No, Monny, I can't."

"So, what do you want? It's the cereal guy, isn't it? You done a profile workup yet?" Barnett gave her the chart along with a synopsis of each killing. She looked up. "Don't just sit there watching me read. Feed my animals. Their bowls are prepared and marked. Match the bowl numbers with the cages. Just put the food next to the cages. They'll reach through and take it. Be careful you don't get scratched."

Barnett sat still.

"Go on. I'll be done by the time you are. Go!"

By the fifth cage, he had learned how to sneak the bowl from below the monkey's eye level up to where the animal least expected it. Sometimes the back, sometimes the front, sometimes the side of the cage. This way the monkey couldn't pull on the bowl as it approached, making a mess. Listening to the slurping of fifteen happy monkeys, Barnett washed his hands then returned to Monny's office.

"I see you figured it out."

"What?"

"How to feed them. Usually my intern does it, but he didn't come in today. You saved me the trouble."

"You're welcome," said Barnett, making a face like he had just sucked a lemon.

"Well ... I think you're right on about the control/power type. It's almost textbook, but you want to know what it means, don't you? The part with the woman is a nice kicker. Different. Okay, first things first. How much weight do you give the organized, disorganized stuff? We once had a big discussion about that, didn't we?"

"Argument was more like it."

"I remember. Tell you what, I'll just say it and you can accept or reject. Your choice."

"Do it."

"I agree that the scenes are organized. Let's add that to our control type and see what we get." Monny walked around the room, looking up at the ceiling. She began to lecture like a college professor.

"The control type gets his excitement from exerting complete control over the life of his victims. The kick is from knowing that he has the power to do whatever he wishes to another human being. Don't misunderstand, Mike, he's not psychotic. He lives in the real world, knows all the rules of society but chooses to ignore them. He lives by his own code."

She looked out her window at the animals, then back at Barnett. "He personalizes the victims and has controlled conversations with them."

"During the crime?" Barnett asked.

"Yes. He's in a very composed, rigid, but still highly stressed state. He uses restraints on the victims, of course."

She looked again at Barnett's notes.

150

"The first two were found in their houses, right?"

"Right."

"The last by the memorial. And that's where the rest are going to be. Isn't that what he said?"

"'Where everyone could see them' were his exact words."

"That's a break from the usual organized behavior pattern, but it doesn't worry me. You?"

"Nope. Special anomaly."

"Agreed. I'd guess he's cool, suave even. High IQ. The writing style of his letters indicates good education. Skilled or white-collar work. Government or government-related work's always a good guess around this area. I'd say he makes a good living. He's socially competent, good negotiator, good at parties. People think he's clever and droll. Possibly good-looking. Dresses nicely. Might be married or have a steady girlfriend. No rapes, right?"

"No evidence of sexual activity at all."

"That could be because of the woman. I can't say whether she accompanies him or not. I'd say probably yes, at least for part of it. When he dumps the bodies, for instance, she might drive the car. We'll talk about her later. Okay . . . I'd say he's high in the birth order of the family, maybe a sibling or two. That's consistent with control types. Upbringing? Let's say inconsistent childhood discipline maybe leaning toward stern. Might have been hit, maybe chronic or severe. Father had a stable job. Mother probably worked. Most important thing about his childhood experience was a feeling of inadequacy and powerlessness. It might be real or perceived."

Monny continued to walk around the room. "Good mobility is always a consistent trait with control and organized types. He won't have a clunker. If he's rich, I'd say a luxury car, Cadillac,

151

Lincoln. Keeps it immaculate, just like his clothes and his grooming."

"Tell me more about the other member of the team."

"That's a toughie. We don't know much about women murderers. They're still a novelty. I'd say these two are very much in love, and, ahem, have great sex. Usually, women accomplices are part of a hedonistic-type team. The thrillseeker category. The men have sex with the victims while she watches. She might even participate. I don't see any of that here. What I do see is that they play the game together. They share the exuberance of catching, controlling and," she hesitated, "making your life miserable. That's a big part of all this for them. Yanking your chain. It's a major component of their power trip."

"I know."

"There's something else you should know. This type often keeps records. It's part of their compulsion. They may videotape the murders, photograph them, keep a journal, something like that. I remember a case where the killer taped the screams of victims and played them back over and over. Your guy, I would guess, keeps a scrapbook or video collection of the media coverage. Anything taken from the victims?"

"Not that we know of."

"Often, they'll take a totem or souvenir of the event. Sometimes a body part to help them relive the moment. Remember Ed Gein, the killer they patterned the movie *Psycho* after? He kept his mother's cadaver for years and made lamp shades out of the skins of his other victims. He wove bracelets out of their hair. And Jerry Brudos. He raped and murdered women, cut off their feet and took them home. He said he killed again and again in his mind by dressing the feet up in heels and masturbating on them. Your man does the same thing but by giving something, not taking. All he has to do is look at a box of cereal in his house. That's enough to get him off."

"Why cereal?"

"Several reasons. Obviously, it's the serial, cereal thing. He did it to show that he knows his stuff, that he could invade your world. A show of control. Few people outside of law enforcement know that joke. Second, it's a simple trademark like a gang spraying a wall. Although he knew it would be made public sooner or later it still belongs to him, and he's terrified of copycats using it. Now that it's been in the media, I don't know what he'll do. He might leave something else in addition to cereal just to show you that a murder was really his. Something only you and he know about. As for why it's cereal and not a different item, you won't know until you learn about his background. It's something from his past, something dark and secret."

"What's next for him, Monny?"

"More of the same. He's not going to move on. That's for sure. He wants to beat you, control you. Intellectually, that is. He won't stop until you say uncle or he's dead. I'll bet my last buck on it."

Chapter 30

The letter carrier left his white Pinto with red and blue stripes double-parked as he bounced up the stairs, two at a time, to deliver a Special Delivery envelope to "A. Sleser, apartment 3B." For an instant, he halted in mid-step wondering if he had locked the car door. *Hell, nobody's going to mess with it.* He laughed it off and continued. He spied the top step and, with a leap worthy of a broad jumper, made it to the landing. He wasn't even winded as his big shoe hit the ground with a thud that echoed through the hallway.

He guessed the apartment was to the left and was correct. "Today is my lucky day," he muttered as he knocked on the door with five quick jabs. No answer. Another flurry of raps. He checked the address on the envelope, impatiently hopping from one foot to the other. He heard shoes on a wooden floor accompanied by a woman's voice singing: "Coming. Coming." A few more steps. "Who's there?"

"Mailman. Special Delivery for Sleser."

"Can you leave it outside the door?"

"Sorry, ma'am. You gotta sign for it."

The peephole opened and she took in his enthusiastic, eager face, bopping, moving up and down, his fingers tapping the envelope in time to a music score in his head.

She opened the door and saw the envelope fall as a hand plunged for her wrist. She jerked her arm but couldn't shake him. She backed into the apartment, the two joined in a crude tango. His foot kicked the door closed behind him.

She saw his eyes widen, his face beam, as he produced a small syringe. He pulled the protective cover with his teeth and spit it out. He pulled on her arm, squeezing until the green-blue of her veins showed through the stretched skin.

The needle slid into her forearm, and she collapsed immediately.

With the body hidden under canvas mail sacks, he drove around the block several times to make sure nobody saw him pull the car into the garage. Dusk helped. So did his facility with the remote-control gadget that closed the door precisely as the hatchback cleared the entrance.

He would wait until dark before he carried her into the house. The drug would last several more hours at least. Now, all he wanted to do was get out of that nasty uniform, change himself back into Harlan Wolfe, and mix a proper Cajun martini.

He hung the uniform in his closet. He was especially fond of it because he had the car to go with it. A total package. It was an easy acquisition, really. After Ralph Nader came down on Pintos for exploding during rear-end collisions, used-car lots were floating with them. Some paint, numbers decal, and a handcrafted government license plate were all that was needed. Sometimes he and Marybeth drove it downtown to shop. Nobody ever ticketed a postal service vehicle as it completed its appointed rounds.

He stood in the bedroom nude, deciding what to wear. He hoped that Marybeth wouldn't see the present he had for her. Probably not. She would just pull the Jaguar in next to the Pinto; no reason to lift up the car cover that kept neighborhood eyes at bay.

"Harlan, I'm home." Her purse, groceries thumped the kitchen counter. "I'm home, Where are you?" she yelled. Marybeth walked into the living room, kicked her high heels off, and ran her soles across the thick textures of the white rug. She spotted the fixings for a martini on the rolling wet bar and grinned as she prepared one for herself.

She took it over to the couch, sank in, and drank. It went to her head immediately, and she drifted off, savoring the cool softness of satin pillows against the nape of her neck. Her rest was short-lived, however. She opened her eyes a few minutes later when she heard someone in the hall.

"Marybeth Wolfe?"

"How did you—?"

"The door was open. I rang the button, but I guess you didn't hear me."

"It broke yesterday. Who are you?" Marybeth said, her voice full of fear.

He produced a badge and ID. "Detective Dave Preemo. I've got some questions. Can we talk here?" She could see the bulge of his pistol through his coat.

Marybeth kept a cautious and confused face as she got up. "What's this about?" she said. "Uh, please sit down."

"Thank you. I'm investigating the murder of a woman who lives in this neighborhood. I'd like to ask you a few questions."

"You don't think I had anything to do with it. Do you?"

"Like I said, we're just checking out leads. Records

157

show you have a green Jaguar."

"That's right."

"Do you remember where you were Wednesday night last week, around eight o'clock?"

"Why yes, I do. I worked late that night and didn't get home until around nine. I was exhausted, had a glass of wine, and went right to sleep."

"Were you alone?"

"As a matter of fact, I was," she said. "My husband was out of town on business."

"Can anyone verify that you were here and—"

"Are you calling me a liar, Detective Preemo?"

"No, no, ma'am," he said contritely.

"I don't think I like your tone. I'm going to ask you to leave." She stood up and nodded towards the door.

"Sorry, ma'am, I can't go. Not 'til I'm finished."

"I think you are finished," she said sternly. "Go before I call your supervisor." She reached for the phone.

"I don't think that's a good idea," he said as he twisted her wrist until she dropped the handset.

"Stop. You're hurting me!"

"You haven't felt anything yet." He threw her on the couch and her legs shot up in the air exposing her thighs. Marybeth tried to slap his face, but he caught her hand. "Now, now," he said, as if she were a child.

He lunged for her chest, ripped open her blouse. She was wearing a black bra which he savagely pulled down. Marybeth tried to fight back, but he was too close. She had no room to swing her arms. He brought his mouth down and began to suck her nipples. Marybeth pounded on his back, dug into the flesh with her long nails. He yelped and bit her breast until she stopped.

The two crashed on the floor, her tattered dress

158

now in a heap beside them. He unbuckled his pants.

"This is what you want, isn't it?" he screamed.

"No, no . . ."

Suddenly, her face turned from terror to bliss. She laughed.

As they climaxed simultaneously, Harlan Wolfe thought about Ann Sleser, apartment 3B.

The best was yet to come.

Chapter 31

Rick Henkel had just finished typing "Michael OR Mike Barnett AND detective AND Washington" into the computer keyboard. By using AND/OR qualifiers, the computer would scan the Nexis database of newspapers and magazines for any stories containing the name Mike or Mike Barnett that also contained the words *detective* and *Washington*. In this way, he was assured of finding material about his particular Barnett and not some yokel with the same name who made the paper because he croaked in a freak steel plant accident.

The screen blinked twice before revealing that it had located seven stories. Henkel pressed the PRINT key and waited.

Since his abrupt meeting with Barnett at the Douglas house, Henkel was beginning to despise the man. It wasn't a deep abhorrence, more like an annoyance, for Barnett represented the only person standing between him and access to the killer. Henkel decided that if he gave the killer some information about Barnett, some little tidbit he could use, then the killer might be inclined to do business.

As the printer spit out paper, Henkel thought how

he would set the killer up so that his face wouldn't be seen, how he could manipulate the lighting, the shadows to hide his features yet let the viewer see that this man was dangerous. "He has killed three women, ladies and gentlemen, and he promises to kill again. What's behind this reign of terror? We'll find out after this message." Henkel smiled as he grabbed the softly folded pile and began reading.

The later stories about the current murders were of no interest. Henkel scanned them and threw them away. He read with great attention, however, a story in the *Washington Post* five years ago about a young detective who was given special permission to question his brother, a convicted felon. The story was short, only a few paragraphs and contained a new name.

Henkel sat in front of the keyboard again and typed: Frank Barnett AND murder. Blink. Blink. One story.

VIET VET CONVICTED
IN CHINATOWN MURDER
by Stephen Monroe
Washington Post *Staff Writer*

After two days of deliberation, a jury convicted a Vietnam veteran of the murder of a prostitute whose body was found in a Chinatown hotel.

Diane Kuan, 27, of Silver Spring, was found dead on February 19th in a third-floor room of the Metro Hotel on H St. NW. Police said they found Frank Barnett, 36, lying unconscious over her body. The medical examiner's office said Kuan died of a blow to the head.

Barnett pleaded innocent to the charges, saying he had met Kuan in a bar, and they agreed to meet later in the lobby of her hotel and go out for dinner. He testified that he went to her room after she failed to come to the lobby.

At his trial, Barnett offered no explanation for how Kuan died. He said the door to her room was open, and she was lying on the bed. He claimed he was struck from behind while examining her.

Barnett denied knowing that Kuan was a prostitute with a history of three arrests for soliciting.

Police said they were not able to verify Barnett's story of an unknown assailant despite a massive search that included the convicted man's brother, a District detective. At the time of the investigation, Detective Mike Barnett was assigned to the homicide squad but was not permitted to actively pursue the case because of his relationship to the suspect.

However, Barnett voluntarily took a leave of absence to pursue his own investigation. Homicide Captain Bertram Wilson said: "The police department does not condone or sanction his actions, but we have no jurisdiction over any private citizen and that was Detective Barnett's status during his leave. We understand Detective Barnett's personal distress in the matter and sympathize with him."

Barnett's attorney Gerard Kuckrowsky said he will appeal the conviction which carries a maximum sentence of life imprisonment. Kuckrowsky will appeal on grounds that the prosecution introduced prejudicial testimony of a "Mai-Lai type" incident that involved Barnett while he was in the military. Barnett served one year in Vietnam with the Army's First Air Cavalry.

Henkel reread the story, highlighting in yellow marker the parts which he planned to tell the killer when he called.

He only had to wait until the following day.

"Mr. Henkel. You know who this is?"

"Yes."

"Do you want to make sure, like last time, or are you positive you know who I am?"

"Saying what you just said is proof enough."

"I knew I had chosen someone intelligent to deal with."

Henkel almost dropped the phone. *He said "to deal." Oh, baby. He went for it.* "When can I put you on TV to tell the whole world your story?"

The voice was clear and calm. "We'll meet tonight and set the ground rules and the date. How does that sound to you, Mr. Henkel?"

"How does it sound? It sounds perfect!"

"Very well. Meet me by the fish market. Nine p.m."

Fish market. Henkel didn't know Washington had a fish market. "I'll be there."

The voice disappeared, and Henkel once again broke open his map book.

Chapter 32

"Fish market? You sure that's what he said?"

"Want to hear it yourself?" said Caggiano, holding a cassette in his hand.

"No. I believe you." Barnett stood in front of a large metropolitan map which hung like a shade. He ran his fingers over the glossy surface. "Seems easy enough to cover. Let's get Harbor and Helicopter Branch in."

"Done." Caggiano made several quick phone calls and returned to Barnett who was still staring at the map. "You're all set. This is getting to be like a police department on TV. The cooperation is becoming awesome."

"Harbor. Molnar."

"This is Barnett, Homicide. We meet again."

"Another joy ride in my future?"

"Could be. What'll it take to secure the channel above and below the fish market?"

"Got a flounder selling drugs?"

"I wish. What'll it take?"

"Do you know what kind of vessel we're dealing with?"

"No. Don't even know if there'll be any vessels. I'm covering all angles."

"The guy with the cereal?"

"Yes."

"No sweat, Barnett. We can handle it. The channel's our jurisdiction, but we can get support from Park Police if we need it."

"Not unless we have to. The fewer people who know the better."

"Okay. When?"

"Tonight. We're meeting three o'clock at headquarters for a briefing."

Barnett didn't hang up the phone, just pressed the button for another line. He called Helicopter Branch stationed at National Airport, told them he wanted Juneau available for tonight. The sergeant who answered said he had already gotten the all clear from downtown, and he'd attend the meeting.

A large map of the waterfront area, left over from the Riverfest festival, was thumbtacked to the corkboard. A man's photo was on the side.

Barnett paced while waiting for people to settle down. A walkie-talkie squawked in the background. Caggiano introduced Barnett to the group then stood to the side along with Captain Wilson who had just arrived.

"Sources tell us that the cereal killer plans to be at the fish market tonight." Barnett pointed to the publicity photo of Rick Henkel. "He's going to meet this man. He may look familiar. He's a TV reporter named Rick Henkel and he has a special interest in this case." A low, good-natured boo came from the

166

half-dozen officers.

Barnett laughed with them. "Remember, Henkel isn't wanted for any crime. He's not to be arrested unless he interferes with our work. Keep in mind, however, that he's our strongest link to the killer. We don't want to spook him. I don't have to tell you that if the killer thinks Henkel is being followed, he won't make contact."

First District Sergeant Steve Graham cleared his throat. "Do you know what the killer looks like?"

"Only a general description based on a profile, not an eyewitness. We believe the killer is male, probably twenty-five to forty, most likely white, because the victims were white. There's also speculation he's got a female accomplice. The only description on her is," he looked around, "she's got a good figure." The crowd murmured. Barnett waited a moment and continued. "She is thought to drive a green car, unknown make and model.

"I want Henkel tailed as soon as he nears the fish market. The sheets I've passed out contain a description of his POV and that of the TV station's unmarked cars. My guess is that he'll come in his own car. We'll have twenty plainclothes and old-clothes officers in the market, spotters on the roof of the Capitol Yacht Club, the Flagship Restaurant, and the three-ninety-five overpass. We'll have night scopes and cameras." He jabbed the map with his pen. "Units will be posted along Water Street and Maine Avenue where you see the red dots. Juneau will be on standby, and we'll be in control of the water."

He glanced over at Molnar, who nodded back.

"I want one person making a master list of license tags. Every vehicle going in and out."

Sergeant Chip De Moine, Juneau's pilot, chimed in. "What's supposed to happen tonight, Mike? Are they passing something or what?"

"The only thing passing tonight will be information. It may be verbal, or it may be on a piece of paper. We don't know. That's why we can't jump on the first person Henkel talks to. It might be innocent. He might be asking for the time.

"Use One D TAC channel for communications. If there are no other questions . . . ? I want everyone in place by eight."

At eight-thirty, Harlan Wolfe chopped the head off a carp, slit its belly from anus to gills, and rubbed the fish's body onto his white apron. Blood, scales, and bits of guts clung to the coarse material. Once satisfied with the haphazard distribution, he rolled up the smelly garment and placed it in a plastic bag.

He padded into the basement, opened a closet door, and reached up for a white hard hat sitting on a shelf. From the floor he grabbed a pair of thick rubber gloves and heavy black boots. He placed these and the plastic bag into an oversized gym bag that said ADIDAS. Looking at the bag he decided he had everything he needed. "Thanks, Kris. I knew it'd come in handy." He swung it over his shoulder, kissed a dozing Marybeth good-bye, and headed out.

Rick Henkel thought about his dress for quite a while and finally settled on new jeans, a dark plaid shirt and a black knitted tie. Casual newsman chic.

He wondered how the killer would make contact. Would he just come right up and say, "Hello, I'm the

168

cereal murderer," or would he hide in a doorway and say "pssst" until Henkel came to him? The one thing he was sure of was that he was safe. The killer wanted the exposure, the publicity, and wouldn't hurt him. Besides, he only killed women.

Henkel took the computer printouts and shoved them in the inner pocket of his sport coat, going over in his mind what he had rehearsed all afternoon about Barnett's brother. The dead prostitute, the conviction, and the incident in Vietnam that came out during the trial. Information good enough to trade. Maybe good enough to parlay into an on-camera interview.

Barnett sat nervously in the passenger side of a maroon sedan with Maryland tags. District police often registered their undercover cars out of state, and it always amazed Barnett how many people it fooled despite the fact that unmarked cars telegraphed their presence with cheap hubcaps that only police agencies bought and usually a small antenna sticking out of the truck lid.

It was eight forty-five and the task force had been in position for almost an hour. Several officers already were having to duck into one of the nearby restaurants to void themselves of the coffee which was drunk continuously.

Barnett and Caggiano positioned their car past the entrance to the fish market on Maine Avenue. A divided highway, they couldn't be seen by anybody entering the fenced-in market.

It was too dangerous for either of them to actually be near the action. Henkel knew what they both looked like, and chances were good the killer would recognize them as well. Most of the officers inside—prowling the area as buyers, sellers, and workers—were from the District, but standard procedure called for borrowing people from outside jurisdictions. In this case, Wilson had requested and received fresh faces from Alexandria and Arlington.

The fish market consisted of about eight permanently docked boats. They were not in a row but placed around the maze of cement piers shaped somewhat like a huge letter H. When the place wasn't too busy, mainly during the day, customers in the know drove their cars right up to the boats away from the newly installed parking meters.

From these boats, fishmongers sold to crowds who had to lean over the edge, stretching their arms over trays of fish buried in chipped ice or bushels of crabs, to pay. Every so often, a monger would rudely shake the bushels until the crabs responded by scuttling and sliding, locking claws with their neighbors. This showed prospective buyers the goods were still alive and fresh.

While the areas adjacent to the fishing boats were fairly free of debris, the market itself reeked from decaying fish overflowing from dumpsters in the delivery lot. In that lot sat refrigerated trucks called reefers which brought locally caught fish from Chesapeake Bay and out-of-town fish like lobsters and king crab from wholesale markets in Baltimore and New York. The trucks parked as close together as they could before turning off their diesel engines. People who lived on boats in the marina, connected to the fish market by a promenade, frequently complained about the low rumble of the trucks.

Several cinder-block buildings stood in the market as well. During the early morning, attendants in white smocks with metal chain gloves on one hand held fish under running faucets and worked knives on them with surgical precision. Cleaners worked mainly for the fishing boats, gutting hundreds of pounds for the customers who wanted cash-and-carry, but they also supplied the public with fish-cleaning services. If a customer brought an uncleaned fish instead of filets—to save money—they could then bring it inside. The price depended upon the fish's weight, but the customer still came out ahead if he didn't mind waiting in line.

The market was bustling at nine o'clock as fish sellers tried to get rid of as much as they could so as not to have to refrigerate their goods overnight. Shrewd customers took advantage of last call as they made their way from boat to boat haggling for the best prices. Always within pennies around the dinnertime crush, prices among competitors began to widen as closing time approached.

It was during this last-minute buying binge that Henkel appeared. He didn't fit into the crowd of working-class shoppers scurrying for bargains. He walked about like a little boy overwhelmed by a giant department store.

The task force had spotted him as soon as he turned his car into the market. The radio conveyed his every move. Cameras recorded any person who came close, whether they talked to him or not.

Harlan Wolfe was watching Henkel, too, but nobody paid any attention to him. He was dressed in the same manner as other workers—white apron, gloves, and boots—who began cleaning up the area, loading unsold fish back into reefers and freezers and hosing down walkways.

Barnett felt very left out. He and Caggiano were

171

resigned to listening to the action on the radio, trying to picture where Henkel was exactly, and what he was doing based on spotters' reports. Barnett resisted the urge to pick up the microphone and guide his people in the fine art of surveillance. He knew they were all competent, hand-picked, in fact, but he still felt compelled to ask if they saw anything unusual. He so badly wanted to ask: What's Henkel doing now? Did he make contact with anyone? Tell me what's going on, for God's sake!

A spotter on the roof of the Capitol Yacht Club saw something. "Subject appears to be very interested in something at Pruitt's," he said into the walkie-talkie.

Henkel stared at a tray of octopi. He asked an Asian fishmonger, "What is this?" The man, who spoke broken English, looked up from the boat. He spoke quickly: "Yes, yes, very good. Octopus, octopus. Very good, very good. You want? You want?"

"I wouldn't know what to do with them."

"You cook. You cook. You want?"

"How do you make it?"

"Ah . . . You put in—" The man gestured with his hands. "How you say 'broken bread'?"

"Bread crumbs?"

"Yes, yes. You take bread crumbs, put fish in," he rolled his hands, "then you put in frying pan. Very good, very good. You want?"

Officer Phil Nicoletti, dressed in street clothes, brushed back his hair, tucking the earpiece nonchalantly under his collar. He walked slowly to Henkel's side, feigning interest in the octopi. The fishmonger continued to show eagerness in the pending sale, buoyed by the new man he had attracted. He looked at Nicoletti. "You want fish?"

"No, thank you. I'm just looking for now."

172

"Okay, okay," he said quickly then turned back to Henkel. "We close soon. You want buy?" A young boy was already scooping fish from the trays, taking them into the back where they would be kept until the next day.

Henkel waved his hand at the man, shook his head, and strolled away. Nicoletti held his lapel and directed his mouth down. "No contact. Breaking off." With that he walked in the opposite direction from Henkel.

Barnett looked at Caggiano but didn't say a word.

Suddenly, a crowd of about ten black teenagers, most of them wearing "the DC uniform," running suits, slammed the doors of two cars and scampered on the pier. "Let's get us some crabs, man. We're gonna partee!" one of the youths wearing a black beret screamed. He gave a high five to the kid next to him.

The kid responded by dancing, hip hop, rolling his fists around like a drunk fighter shadow boxing. Several of the kids began dancing toward the boats. Then, in an instant, the happy mood changed as the boy with the beret was looking up from a mud puddle.

"You tripped me, motherfucker!"

"You tripped on your own feet, nigger!"

The two boys faced off, cursing, walking in a circle. Their friends cheered them on. Other customers scattered as someone screamed something about a gun.

Barnett tensed when he heard reports of the commotion. "Shit, they're going to fuck it up, Cag!" The radio went silent and Barnett knew what that meant. He called on the air: "Where is he?"

No response. "Damn it, where is he?"

"Went in the direction of the parking lot," Nicoletti said.

"Don't see him," said Graham from the roof.

A spotter on the overpass next to a car with the hood up scanned the streets. "His car's still here," he said.

"Then he has to be here," Barnett said.

Five minutes passed.

"Anything, Molnar?" Barnett asked.

"Nothing. We're the only ones out on the water tonight."

Five more minutes passed.

"I'm gonna do it, Cag." Barnett keyed the mike button. "I want Henkel found. Do whatever it takes."

Startled crews didn't know how to react as men boarded the boats, pirate style, flashing badges, demanding to look around. The reports came in fast.

"Pruitt clear."

"Jesse Taylor clear.

"Custis & Brown clear . . ."

"Who's checking the promenade?" Barnett said.

"Got it," a voice said. "All clear."

"What the fuck—" said the teenager with the beret, choosing the bushel with the most active crabs when an officer elbowed him flying onto the boat. "It's the heat, man. What's happening?"

"Don't know, man," said his sparring partner. "We didn't do nothin' wrong. Just a little misunderstandin'. Let's get our shit and clear out."

"Yeah, man. Give me that funny money we got."

"Fuckin' honky cops—"

Barnett couldn't wait any longer. He and Caggiano stepped out and raced into the truck parking lot. "Seen anybody back here who doesn't belong?" he screamed to a man shoveling chipped ice over fish

174

in a crate. "No, sir," the man responded. "Sure didn't."

Barnett and Caggiano split up and checked the other trucks getting ready to depart.

When Barnett left, the man continued to shovel. He paused, wiped his forehead with a handkerchief, and shuffled over to a wooden lid. He placed it on top of the crate and bound it with wire. He clipped the excess with a wire cutter. He shimmied the crate onto a hand truck and wheeled it over to a van that was idling.

"Hope you're not too cold in there, Mr. Henkel," he said, patting the crate.

Chapter 33

"Welcome to our family," Harlan Wolfe announced to his visitors.

Rick Henkel and Ann Sleser sat on either side of a long dining-room table. Wolfe sat at the head and Marybeth opposite him. The table was formally set with silver flatware, hand-tatted napkins, crystal wine glasses, and two gold candelabra that threw twitching shadows on the walls.

"I trust that you've warmed up, Mr. Henkel. I regret having to extricate you in such a manner, and I heartily apologize for the inconvenience."

"What was it that you—"

"Ether. Out of fashion but effective. It used to be a parlor drug in the last century. People would have ether parties, but I digress." He looked over at Sleser. "I wish to welcome you here too, Ms. Sleser. I trust your stay has been pleasant so far."

Ann Sleser's eyes were dead. Her body sat hunched, barely holding her head up. Although hidden from Henkel's view by the table, she was strapped to her chair by a wide leather belt. She stared briefly at Wolfe, her face trying to understand his words, then retreated to her front-and-center dazed condition.

"Yes, well . . ." Wolfe said.

"What's going on here?" Henkel screamed. "What are you doing?" He started to get up but found his left foot chained to the floor. "What the—?"

"Mr. Henkel, please relax. This will all be clear to you soon enough. By the way, I read the papers in your pocket. Were they supposed to be for me?"

Henkel didn't respond.

"I certainly hope not. You think I don't know all about Detective Barnett and his brother? Please don't insult me."

Henkel sat down. He felt his heart beat faster than ever before. His breathing came in gasps. He thought he was going to hyperventilate. Wolfe noticed.

"Please, Mr. Henkel. No one is going to harm you. I must take precautions. That's the reason for the restraint. It will be removed at the proper time. Please," he said harshly then smiled.

Marybeth finally spoke. "Mr. Henkel," she said softly, putting her hand on his. "Harlan's telling the truth. No one will hurt you. I promise."

Henkel sat back. He tugged on his leg a second time to make certain the chain was secure. Then he watched as Marybeth and Wolfe, without any warning, arose in unison and walked into the kitchen. "Hey," Henkel shouted after them. "What about us?"

He looked across the table at Ann. "You all right? He touched her face trying to snap her out of her befuddlement. "Hey—"

Harlan stormed into the room, approaching Henkel with great speed. He slapped him in the face. "You touched her! What did I tell you about touching her." Crack!

178

"Nothing, I—"

"I don't want to hear any excuses! You touched her face, didn't you?"

Henkel was so stunned by the outburst he couldn't speak.

"Well," shouted Wolfe. "Didn't you?"

"I—" Smack!

"I've had just about enough out of you. You're going to be punished for this!" He stomped into the kitchen.

"We gotta get out of here," Henkel said to Ann. He pulled on the chain with both hands. "These people are crazy—"

Henkel stopped talking when he saw Wolfe return, this time with Marybeth. "Look at him," Wolfe said. "So innocent looking . . ."

Henkel saw the madness in Wolfe's eyes.

Marybeth calmly stood by Henkel, just beyond the reach of his leash. "You didn't touch her, did you? Tell me you didn't," she said.

"All I did was try to get her up, to wake her. I—"

"See!" Harlan screamed. "He admits it. He's got to be punished."

"I'm afraid I can't help you. You did wrong. You know that, don't you?" she said softly.

"All I did was . . . What is going on here? This can't be real. It can't be . . ."

It was after midnight when the task force assembled at headquarters. "What the hell happened tonight?" Barnett shouted as he walked around the room. The fluorescent lights were harsh. "What the hell happened out there?"

Nobody answered.

"I'll tell you what happened. We let a killer get away and our prime lead is missing. That's what happened."

Graham spoke after the echoes of Barnett's voice faded. "It's our fault. We lost him in the commotion with those kids. We fucked up. What else can we say, Mike?" The others in the room concurred under their breaths.

"We're not going to get anywhere, blaming each other," Caggiano injected. "While it's still fresh in our minds, let's go over what occurred."

Each officer in turn told exactly what he observed and heard. It ended with Nicoletti saying that all the boats and buildings were checked. The market was closed off ten minutes after Henkel was out of sight, and the killer or he could have left in any car or truck that exited during those ten minutes without being checked.

"Anything else?" Barnett asked. "I want all the photos developed and the master list of tags checked. I want to know who was behind the ruckus."

"I'll do it," yelled Graham.

"I want all the boats canvassed tonight. Carry a photo of Henkel. See if anyone remembers him."

"Dry land isn't my area, but I'll take care of it," said Molnar.

"You've all got my pager number. Call when you know something."

The crowd dispersed, and Caggiano walked over to Barnett who was gathering his papers. "We had him, Cag. We fucking had him."

"I know, Mike."

"Do you think he knew about the tap, knew we were waiting?"

"Couldn't have. Not unless he saw us, and I

don't think he did. I think he was planning to grab Henkel all along. He caused that disturbance with the kids as insurance against people in the market, not us."

"Are you sure? We still haven't found our leak."

"Get some sleep, Mike. I'll see you tomorrow."

Chapter 34

Over the next two days, reports landed on Barnett's desk one after another. The officers working on them had put in extra hours to dispatch them as quickly as possible. They were trying, in a small way, to make up for the screwup at the fish market.

A check of license tags showed that a white van, which had arrived in the fish market before eight o'clock, was reported stolen several hours before the stakeout. It was found the following day abandoned by RFK stadium and taken directly to the impound lot where Quill went over it.

Barnett was sitting at his desk when Quill walked in with a pile of papers.

"We friends?" Barnett asked.

"Yeah, I guess so. You bought your friendship with a bottle, you slimeball. By the way, scum, the wire you got from Couch Orthopedics matches the one found in Kris Rose's ears." He was about to ask what good it was going to do but stopped. He didn't want to fight that fight again.

"Thanks. What about the van?"

Quill related how the van was loaded with T-shirts, sweatshirts, baseball caps, visors, and cheap souvenirs. The owner came to the impound lot and checked the contents against his invoice. Nothing had been taken since that afternoon, but something had been added. He didn't know how a pair of shoes had gotten there. They weren't his.

"I've got the shoes, but I don't know what to do with them," said Quill. "They're just everyday black loafers. Nothing special. Why would our guy leave a pair of shoes around?"

"Good question. Obviously, he didn't walk around barefoot so he must've had some other kind of footwear."

"One other thing," said Quill. "Some of the clothing in the back of the van was damp. The owner said the truck didn't leak, so we can presume the killer put something wet in the back."

Barnett rubbed his chin and looked up. "Shit, I don't know. You going over it again?"

"No, I've sucked it clean. I'd like to give it back to the guy. He's just barely making a living selling junk to the tourists."

"Release it when you're ready. And Joe . . . thanks again."

"Don't worry, you'll get my bill."

The phone rang, and it was Graham. "We found the black kids who were fighting in the fish market. You're not gonna believe this: they said somebody came up to them when they were hanging out in Hains Point and gave them two hundred bucks to party. The only thing was that they had to buy a couple of bushels of crabs and make a commotion in the market. What are they gonna say, 'No'?"

"Could they describe him?

"What him? It was a her. White. Said she was a fox, wore tight jeans, good ass . . ." Barnett felt a shock. He knew who that woman was. ". . . knitted hat over

184

her hair. They didn't see her car. She gave them the cash and told them to split. They were half-stoned at the time."

"Any of the money left?"

"They said they spent it all, but who knows? I ran into Molnar at the market. He said to tell you that spreading the photo of Henkel around netted a big zero except for that Asian fish seller. He's got a few more people to check, guys who didn't come into work yesterday. He'll send the paperwork along, but he wanted you to know what's happening."

"Thanks, Graham."

Barnett spun around when he heard Caggiano's voice. "Mike, Jim Sherman's here to see you."

Caggiano presented Sherman, general manager of WJLA, Henkel's station. Barnett and he had spoken on the phone the day before. He had told Sherman that Henkel's car was found outside the fish market after it had closed and that several people had spotted him by the boats. Barnett didn't mention anything about Henkel's planned meeting with the killer.

Sherman was dressed in a gray conservative business suit with a handkerchief in the breast pocket. His face was very wrinkled, even though Barnett figured his age to be mid-forties at the most. Barnett noticed that Sherman's hand trembled as they shook.

"What can I do for you, Mr. Sherman? I'm sorry, but we don't have anything new to tell you about Mr. Henkel's disappearance."

"Is there some place we can talk privately?"

"Certainly, come in here. Is it okay for Lieutenant Caggiano to join—"

"Of course, I didn't mean—"

Barnett put his arm around Sherman's shoulder. "Are you all right?"

"Yes . . . Well . . . nothing like this has ever happened before. I mean, I've been in the news business for twenty-five years, I've covered wars, fires. I've seen people die in front of me, but nothing like this, I—"

"Please come inside," said Barnett, holding the door open to the interrogation room. "Can I get you something?"

"No, I'm okay." Sherman produced a videotape cassette and placed it on the table. "This came today. Here's the envelope in case you need it." Sherman took a deep breath and continued. "We played it at the station and it's—you'll see."

"I'll call Quill," said Caggiano as he rushed out of the room.

Sherman sat back. "We encouraged Rick to work on the story. We really thought it was going to be good for the station and for Rick, too. We didn't think it would come to this. Rick always said he wasn't scared, and we didn't think there was anything to worry about, either. We were wrong, Detective Barnett."

"I've seen this several times, Monny, but I'd like your opinion," Barnett said.

"Damn it, Barnett. Am I going to lose my lunch?"

"I'll buy dinner if you do."

Dr. Monika Sidor took the tape and inserted it into the VCR in the conference room near her laboratory. She walked to a seat next to Barnett, fiddled with the remote control unit and the two watched as the TV screen turned from gray to color.

Both were nude on a white rug. The wall behind them was white. Rick Henkel lay on top of Ann Sleser. Sweat dripped down the side of his face into

186

stubble. "I love you," he said mechanically.

He began pumping up and down. Ann showed no emotion. She held onto his back with only the slightest grip. As Henkel drew his body up, her hand slid off, and she moved it back as if it were a robot arm in a factory. "I love you," he repeated without enthusiasm, "but they won't let us be." He looked up and over Ann's head, continuing to pump vigorously.

Faintly, a voice off camera whispered, "Good, good."

"I love you. I love you. Why won't they leave us alone if we love each other?"

"Excellent," the voice whispered.

Henkel's eyes were trained straight ahead. He squinted, spoke slowly, deliberately. Paper rustled in the background. "We can run away together, you and me. They'll never know."

"They'll know." A woman's voice seemed to come from Ann, but her lips weren't moving. They were parted but lifeless.

"What should we do?" said Henkel groaning, trying to keep pumping, his face full of pain and pleasure.

"We will kill them. We will kill them and—"

Henkel's face strained. "I—I can't stop it, it's—"

"No!" the other voice whispered. "No, not yet!"

Suddenly, the screen went black. The TV made a raspy noise.

Monny pressed the button and the machine went quiet. She and Barnett sat in the dark without talking for about a minute. Then Monny got up and switched on the light.

"Whew, Mike. What kind of sickness is that?"

"I've got my theories, but I'm here for your opinion."

"Jesus, Barnett. Who are those two and where did

you get that tape?''

Barnett explained about the fish market and Henkel's kidnapping. He said he didn't know who the woman in the video was, but they were almost certain the tape came from the killer.

"Rewind it while I get a notepad. I want to see it again," Monny said.

As they sat in the dark, the light of the screen flickering into their eyes, Barnett watched disgust in Monny's face turn into one of detached concentration. When it was over, she had filled two pages with notes.

"Here's what I think. Henkel and whoever that woman was were play-acting. Well, Henkel was. She was out of it, drugged probably. It's obvious he was reading some sort of script."

Barnett nodded.

"Right," said Monny. "That's obvious. If that was the killer in the background, the male voice we heard, I'd say he was having them act out a special scene. Maybe something from his past. Exactly what, I can't tell you, but something traumatic."

Monny stood and began to walk around the room. She looked at Barnett. "There's a wild card in all of this, Mike. That traumatic incident that I just told you about. It might not have ever happened. It may have all been some fantasy. All in his imagination."

"So you're saying that it either happened or it didn't. Is that supposed to help me?"

"You get what you pay for."

"Sorry. Assuming it was a real incident, why would he act it out?"

"Two reasons. Well, let me back up. These reasons would hold even if it wasn't a real incident. Even if it's a fantasy, it's real to him." Monny pushed up her lab coat sleeves. "One, by playing it over, he might be able to come to grips with the trauma. Two, by acting it out, he might be able to change the outcome—at least in his mind—by having the actors change the original lines."

"Like getting rid of nightmares."

"Precisely. It's quite the treatment these days, therapists telling patients to have the dream again and change the ending." Barnett thought about Frank's recurring dream of the devil woman who burned him with her fingers. "You can do it if you put your mind to it. In this case, judging from the script, I'd say that what you see is what you get. He may have been in love with someone who his or her—let's not leave her out—family didn't approve of."

"That's traumatic enough to warrant something like this?"

"You bet your ass it is. To some people, especially unstable people."

"What about the 'let's kill them' part? Do you think they actually killed someone?"

"Don't know. It might be true, or it might be the part of the dream he's recasting. Maybe he wants to kill them. Whoever 'they' are."

"How does this tie into the other women he killed?"

"I'm still guessing, but it's possible that instead of Henkel in the top role—pardon the expression—he may have played himself with those women."

"But there was no sign of sexual assault in those cases. Maybe he couldn't get it up, huh? Too painful."

"Right on. It may have turned out to be more painful than he expected. Out of frustration he murdered the women. Normally, he's okay sexually, but not when he's acting out this particular scene. That could be why he brought in an outsider. Unfortunately, your Mr. Henkel didn't have the necessary staying power to finish the job."

"Does that mean our man will try it again?"

"Maybe. Or he may decide that this arrangement doesn't work and he'll go back to doing it himself until he finds the right partner to finish the scene. Remember, he's a power type. Unless he obtains absolute control over a situation, does exactly what he wants to do, he's not satisfied. He couldn't get control over Henkel. That's for sure."

"Okay, Monny. Here's the part I really don't get at all. Why send the tape if it wasn't exactly what he wanted? And why send it to the station?"

Monny thought for a minute. "He sent it to the station for publicity. He wants the media to know he's still around. He also knew they'd send it to you."

"But then I'd know he wasn't perfect, that he hadn't succeeded."

"Yes, but he also knew that you'd be sitting somewhere trying to figure it out, expending time, energy, and mental anguish." Monny put down her pencil. "He's exerting control over you then. Isn't he, Mike?"

Chapter 35

"This is getting to be a nasty habit, Mike. And it's scaring away the tourists."

"It's not one of my favorite things either, Ted."

"He's that Henkel guy, isn't he?" Green asked.

"Was."

"Who's the woman?"

"Haven't a clue."

The two were standing at the top of the Lincoln Memorial, their backs to the massive marble steps that led to the reflecting pool, the Mall, and the Washington Monument. In the distance, the Capitol dome was reflecting a rising orange sun.

They looked up at the huge statue of the sixteenth president who sat as if presiding over the perverse offering at his feet.

"When did the call come in?" Barnett asked as he studied the red puddle that had covered the white marble floors like a thin layer of jelly.

"Around dawn. Usual morning rounds. And you know who found it?" Green said, his eyebrows lifting.

"Don't tell me . . ."

"Yep. Travis. The same attendant who found that

woman by the Vietnam memorial. He asked for a different job and got the morning cleanup at the Lincoln. What does that say about life, Mike?"

Barnett studied the two bodies that were frozen in a hideous act of love. Their noses, eyes, and mouths seemed to melt into each other's face. And where their torsos met, Barnett could discern a seamless red line from their chests to their hips. The legs meshed. Hers, his, hers, his.

Their arms were fully extended, spread-eagle style with fingers clasped tightly, wrists bound with wire. Barnett knew it was special wire.

In the small of Henkel's back, on a mat of blood-soaked hair, emerged an uneven mound of Grape Nuts.

Some morsels had already blown away and adhered to the sticky marble floor like walnut bits on a caramel apple.

"He still around?"

"He's in the office, probably filling out his retirement papers. I've got his statement."

Barnett rubbed his forehead. He looked at his watch and reached for his notebook. "I'll get it from you later."

Quill appeared at the top step trying to catch his breath. "Whew. That's quite a walk." He spotted the dead lovers. "Looks familiar."

Green glanced over at Quill, trying to make sense of his statement. He started to ask but decided to say hello instead.

Quill greeted him and pulled a cup of coffee from his bag. He punched a hole in the plastic top with a pen and proceeded to drink, never taking his eyes off the embracing couple.

"This is getting bad, Mike. I highly recommend you catch this guy," he said, looking over the cup.

192

Quill's attempt to take the edge off the situation fell flat when Barnett didn't respond. Quill shrugged and put his coffee cup down on the floor away from the immediate area and began taking pictures, spiraling inward until he had shot an entire roll. "You can touch now," he said to Barnett after he pressed the automatic rewind button.

Barnett didn't move. He stood there thinking about what Monny said. *Control. He knows exactly what I'm doing now.*

"Go ahead, Mike. I'm done," Quill shouted.

As if to defy the killer's hold, Barnett walked towards the dead couple very slowly. *See, you bastard, I'm taking my time.* He snapped on surgical gloves and proceeded to unwrap one set of wires. He dropped it in a plastic bag that Quill held open. Then the other set. Slowly, unwinding, dropping it in another bag.

Standing up, Barnett motioned to Quill who was putting on gloves. "Sure you don't want to wait for the medical examiner's men?" Quill asked.

"No. Give me a hand."

The bodies made a sucking sound when they lifted Henkel by his stiff arms off the woman and slid him down by her feet. Her belly oozed from stab wounds. They turned Henkel over, his eyes still open, his mouth agape. His penis and testicles had been slashed, his torso stabbed.

"Okay," said Barnett breathlessly.

Quill made a close examination then stood up and shook his head solemnly at Barnett. They covered the bodies and waited inside the wales which wrapped around the majestic columns.

Quill picked up his coffee cup and made a sour face. "Cold." He sipped anyway. He and Barnett stood looking over the mall which was just coming

193

to life with joggers running along the dirt paths on either side. "The wires were tied post mortem," Quill said with little emotion. "Didn't see anything else, but I'll—"

"The medical examiner's boys are coming up the elevator. You done here?" Green asked.

"Yeah, Ted. Would you do me a favor? Would you ask your people if they saw anything last night?"

"Sure Mike, but vehicles aren't permitted on the driveway." He pointed down the stairs. "If we saw someone we would have checked them out. I'll ask around though. Sometimes we just tell lost tourists to move on."

The stacked gurneys clanked as they were pushed off the elevator into the open rotunda.

Barnett and Quill walked down the steps. The morning chill was burning off.

"They got an elevator here? Shit," Quill said. "You going back?"

"No. I've got an errand to run. I'll see you later."

Barnett crossed the Memorial Bridge onto Route 395. The heavy morning traffic had not yet started going into the city, but the Pentagon parking lot was almost full. He turned off his two-way radio, made sure his pager was operating, and swung down Route 95 to Lorton.

Chapter 36

Barnett drove away from Lorton with his brother's face stuck in his mind. All he could think of was his plea.

"Help me, Mike."

Barnett drove with the windows opened; a cool breeze filtered through. In one quick move, he picked up the microphone out of habit and brought it to his mouth. He'd been out of pocket for several hours. Then he stopped, slid it back into its holder. He aimlessly drove around the Virginia countryside.

Supercop Barnett they call him. Barnett, who squeezes dry leads until they became evidence. Barnett, who surprises his colleagues with his facility to slip between the dirty streets and sophisticated crime labs. Barnett, who they call in to find murderers after everyone else fails.

They don't know the other Barnett, the one who has failed to solve the most important case of his life. The Barnett who can't find the street punk who killed a prostitute in Chinatown.

The one man who could set his brother free.

Barnett pulled into a cinder-block roadhouse. The place was smokey and close. He ordered a double

Black Jack and beer chasers.

He didn't arrive home until after dark.

Carol and Penny were sitting at the kitchen table over cups of hot chocolate when he walked in the door.

Barnett didn't try to hide his fatigue as Penny jumped and wrapped her arms around his neck. With Penny hanging on, he kissed Carol.

"We're glad you're home," Penny yelped.

"Well, I'm glad to be home. How was your day?"

"It was great. Wanna see what I made in school?"

Carol eyed him suspiciously. "Maybe Daddy would like something to drink first."

"What do you want, Daddy?"

"How about some juice."

Penny walked to the refrigerator, took out a container of orange juice, and poured a glass.

"Thanks. Now, what did you do at school? Let's see."

"I'll be right back," Penny said, running to her bedroom.

"And how was your day?" Carol said, mimicking his tone.

He took a long swallow and told her about seeing Frank.

"Mike, stop torturing yourself. There's nothing you can do about—"

Penny interrupted the conversation. "Look, Daddy." She showed him a red and white pot holder with blue lines. "Mrs. Wilkins said it was the most colorful pot holder she's ever seen."

"It sure is beautiful."

"I'm going to keep it for my oven."

"Okay, Pen. I said you could stay up to see Daddy, but it's late. Let's go."

Penny looked up and pouted. "Mommy says you

196

have to work late at the office, Daddy. Are you on a case?"

"Who told you about cases?"

"Mommy said it's when you catch criminals."

"I'm on a case right now. It's an important one, but not as important as seeing you. I'll be home the regular time tomorrow. Okay?"

Carol shot him a dirty look.

"Let's go. We'll be in to kiss you good-night in five minutes. Five minutes," Carol said. Penny disappeared.

"I wish you wouldn't do that," Carol said.

"Do what?"

"Promise you'll be home early. You're not here to see her when she's disappointed."

"Who says I won't be here?"

"Mike—"

"It's going to be a day or two before they identify the woman they found at the Lincoln. I'll be able to break away early tomorrow."

She softened her face. "Tell me about Frank."

"I'm trying to get him to see the psychiatrist more often, but I can't force him. When he looks at me and begs for help I—"

"You've done everything you can. You know that. Deep down, even Frank knows it."

"It's not only that, it's . . . it's my fault that Dad . . . I'm to blame . . ."

They talked long into the night, planning to sleep late the next morning, but the call from the medical examiner woke Barnett at seven-thirty. He spoke softly, trying not to wake Carol.

"Breasts? What are you talking about?" Barnett rubbed the crud out of his eyes and picked up the clock to check it again. "She had implants? What— Really?" Barnett snapped up, now alert. "Really?"

197

He started to laugh then remembered her dead body underneath Henkel and stopped. He looked at the clock again. "I'll be down soon."

He got out of bed, stretched, and rubbed his back. "How do you like that? Learn something new every day," he mumbled.

From under the covers, a sleepy voice said: "What did you learn already?"

"Sorry. It was the medical examiner's office." Carol peeked out. "The woman they found at the Lincoln. She had breast implants." Carol opened both eyes and focused on her husband. "According to the ME, I should be able to trace the woman's identity from the implants."

Carol was now awake. "Mike."

"Yeah, babe."

"You have a weird job."

"I know. That's why you love me." He tumbled back to the bed and kissed her.

"That's just one of the reasons."

Chapter 37

Barnett drove to the medical examiner's office in the DC General Hospital complex. He was tired, but the thought of learning someone's identity from breast implants recharged him. He parked his car and walked in the building.

Dr. Charles Yun-Li greeted Barnett with a firm handshake and a cheery hello. Yun-Li was Acting Medical Examiner; the city hadn't filled the top position for more than a year since the previous head left to become ME in Connecticut. The ME's office had been in a state of chaos trying to keep up with the record number of homicides mainly caused by drug-related murders. Although Yun-Li did an outstanding job, he wasn't asked to take over the position. He was of the wrong political stripe. It was rumored he had been offered jobs in Chicago, Los Angeles, and Miami and was studying his options.

"I did not do the actual autopsy, Detective Barnett," he said. "Dr. Samuel Peele did it. He is a very capable man."

The two walked down the hallway, which smelled of antiseptic.

"Mr. Quill was here yesterday taking fingerprints from the woman. I do not know the status of his work." Yun-Li spoke in a stiff, official manner.

"There's probably no record of her prints, otherwise I would have heard from him already."

"Then I am glad I can help you." Yun-Li pointed to a lab-room door. "In here. Yes?"

Barnett had been inside many times, and it always reminded him of a lab from college. Long tables with thick black stone tops, Bunsen burners, ventilation hoods. Several white-coated people hunched over the tables twirled test tubes above blue flames.

Yun-Li walked over to a burnished metal table that had a kidney-shaped, stainless steel container on top. He presented its contents to Barnett. "This is a breast implant which we removed from the woman. It contains a silicone-based jelly." Barnett held it in his palms. He moved his fingers up and down like a flitting butterfly. It felt firmer than he had expected.

Yun-Li cleared his throat. "Some months ago I had read a letter in a journal from a medical examiner who learned that breast implants had serial numbers. That's not unexpected when you remember that anything of a manufactured nature of any consequence placed into the body during surgery has serial numbers." He counted on his fingers. "Pacemakers, hip replacements, artificial hearts—" He stopped abruptly. "You understand, yes?"

"So if there's ever a problem—"

"Precisely. Some years ago a certain lot of a manufacturer's pacemakers was recalled. The patients were found through serial numbers registered with their doctors and had the units replaced."

"And the same for breast implants."

"Yes. There have been some terrible tragedies,

200

especially those implanted in the early days. This is not my field, but I understand that there have been instances of leakage." He shuddered. "Terrible, terrible. Why cannot women take what God gives them? I know many people think it is worth the risk, but I cannot understand it."

Barnett shrugged. "Vanity, thy name is woman."

Yun-Li was surprised. "Yes. Just so." He handed Barnett a piece of paper. "The company is based in Denver, Colorado. If you call them, they will help you find the doctor who handled the surgery. From there you can get the patient's name. Yes?"

"Yes."

The company would not give Barnett the surgeon's name over the phone, and it took a personal visit from a friend at Denver PD to pry it loose. The company executive screamed something about confidentiality, but the police officer later told Barnett the phrase "product liability lawsuit" came up, too. The officer assured the jumpy man that the woman died of multiple stab wounds, and it had nothing to do with her designer breasts.

The local doctor was much more helpful, especially after Barnett showed him photographs of the woman, and he too was satisfied as to the cause of death.

"Her name was Ann Sleser," Dr. Jahawaral Gumpta said.

Barnett didn't know it until the doctor told him, but Gumpta was quite well known in the Washington area. He established the Centre for Body Contouring ten years prior and was proud of being the first to advertise nose jobs and tummy tucks on television and radio. "You've seen our commercials, haven't you, Detective? They're done with great dignity and correctness."

As Gumpta talked, Barnett seemed to remember a commercial showing a beautiful woman walking in the park thinking about how great life would be if her outside beauty matched her inner beauty. "That was ours," Gumpta said with a wide smile.

"About Ms. Sleser."

"Oh, yes. She came to me about five months ago. She was dissatisfied with the size and shape of her breasts." Gumpta took off his glasses and ran his fingers through his graying temples which contrasted with his chocolate-colored skin. He tapped the spectacles against the desk blotter and continued. "As we do for all our prospective patients, we explained to her the risks and benefits of cosmetic surgery. In some cases, we ask them to consult with a psychiatrist before engaging our services."

Barnett didn't care about this, but he was curious. "Why is that?"

He spoke softly. "Well, quite candidly, some people don't need us as much as they think they do." He raised his voice to normal. "Of course, beauty is in the eye of the beholder, Detective Barnett, but sometimes we get women who could be on the cover of *Glamour* or *Vogue* and they still find fault with their bodies. They're like anorexics. No matter how skinny they are, they look in the mirror and see a fat person."

Gumpta templed his fingers. "I'm not one to turn away business, but frankly there's no percentage in taking these patients on. We can't improve their looks. About ninety percent of our practice is referrals, and these people can't sell for us if their friends

202

and neighbors don't see a marked difference."

"So you send them to shrinks for being too beautiful?"

Gumpta sat back. "Detective Barnett, I fear you're being sarcastic. You don't like what I do, do you? Many people don't. They think it's frivolous and vain. It doesn't bother me in the least. I make people feel better. Can other professions boast the same thing?"

Barnett looked away then back at Gumpta. "Let's talk about Ms. Sleser."

"She came to me because of dissatisfaction with her breasts, as I said. I examined her and we discussed the various implants available. My associates and I prepared a computer simulation of what she could expect. She liked what she saw and we performed the surgery."

"Did you suggest she see a psychiatrist?"

"No, I did not. It seemed to me that Ms. Sleser was levelheaded, mature, and knew exactly what she wanted and why she wanted it. To be quite clinical, her breasts were out of the average range and augmentation was clearly indicated."

"It might help me, Doctor Gumpta, if you could share with me your psychological evaluation of her. It might contain some information that I could use."

Gumpta balked, then said, "I suppose there's no harm in sharing it with you, now is there?" He called his receptionist on the phone and asked her to bring in copies of specific parts of the file which he referred to by letter. "It will only take a minute."

"You said that ninety percent of your clients are referrals. Can you tell me who referred Ms. Sleser to you?"

"I recall the woman but not her name. Wait . . .

Marybeth something. It will be in the file. It's funny you should ask because she was someone I turned away."

"What was wrong with her?"

"If I remember correctly," he paused and smiled, "absolutely nothing."

Chapter 38

Route 7 in northern Virginia cut a path through one of the nation's newest and fastest growing cities, Tysons Corner. Referred to by locals as just Tysons, it was a city composed entirely of shopping malls and technology parks mainly serving The Beltway Bandits—companies that rely on government contracts. Planners call Tysons an edge or satellite city, an area where people inch along in rush-hour traffic all day, and nobody ever walks except within the confines of a shopping mall.

Barnett hated to admit it, but Washington was losing the population battle to this suburban mass of chrome, glass, and rounded brick facades. The area's best-paying jobs along with some of the finest clubs, restaurants, and bars were choosing this suburb instead of the District.

The buildings all looked the same to him, and Barnett was forced to smooth out the crumpled piece of paper containing directions that he had glanced at and tossed on the car mat. He had reread it several times before he finally located Marybeth Wolfe's office.

As soon as he announced himself to the receptionist, Barnett was ushered in.

She wore a conservative blue business suit with black pumps. Barnett noted that her skin was smooth despite the lack of makeup. Her hair was pulled back severely and knotted into a bun. A jade clip held it in place. Her eyes had only a hint of eye shadow. It was obvious to Barnett that she had dressed down for the office.

She held out her hand to greet him then disappeared behind a mahogany desk which held a pen and pencil imbedded in an onyx base with a silver nameplate. On the wall were several framed watercolors of Paris street scenes.

She leaned her forearms on two perfectly aligned stacks of paper and fluttered her eyelashes as if she were wearing contact lenses. "When you called this morning, I didn't tell you my little secret."

"Secret?"

"We know each other . . . in a way."

Barnett waited.

"I met your wife several weeks ago at a party on the Hill," she finally said. "We chatted for quite a while. I was disappointed that you weren't there. I wanted to meet you."

"I must have been working late."

"That's what Carol said." She opened the lid of an inlaid cigarette box on her desk. "Would you care for one?"

"No, thank you."

"Do you mind if—"

"Please, help yourself."

Thick clouds of smoke drifted towards the ceiling. Barnett waited for her to settle back.

"As I told you on the phone, I'm investigating the death of Ann Sleser."

She shivered. "I read about her and that reporter in

the newspaper. What's this city coming to? The Lincoln Memorial, for goodness sake. It's the work of that serial killer, isn't it?"

"How well did you know Ms. Sleser?"

"I only met her once, at a dinner party. We're invited to many functions. We entertain quite a bit too, as you might expect. We were talking, a group of women, and the conversation turned to cosmetic surgery. One woman told us stories about her liposuction operation. Another had a tummy tuck. Ann asked everyone for their doctor's names, and I referred her to Dr. Gumpta."

"How did you know about Gumpta?"

"The same way. Through a referral. Another cocktail party contact in fact. To be quite honest, I don't remember who it was who told me about him."

"Can you tell me anything about Ms. Sleser? What was she like?"

"All I remember is that she was charming, a bit on the shy side, pretty and," she looked down at her well-endowed chest, "rather flat chested."

"Did she come with anyone?"

"I really don't know." She snatched a piece of notepaper from a holder and scribbled on it. "Here's the name of the person who hosted that party. He probably knew Ann well, although you never know with these parties." She flipped through her Daytimer, copied a number, and handed the slip to Barnett.

"Thanks."

"What will you do now? Will you interview the person whose number I gave you? I mean, what's the next step in the investigation?"

Barnett looked puzzled. No one had ever asked him a question like that.

"This may sound strange, but I've always been

207

interested in police work. I read books about true crime and all. It's fascinating work, I would think."

"It has its moments."

"So? What's next?"

"If you really want to know . . . I'll go through her apartment, try to find anything to link her with her assailant. Then I'll talk to her friends and acquaintances and see what they know."

"Fascinating."

"As I said, it has its moments. Ninety percent of police work is routine, and most of what you learn is irrelevant."

"You mean like talking to me?"

"I wouldn't—"

"It's okay. I'm not insulted although I did give you a lead, didn't I?"

"Yes, you did. We live for the odd fact that will bring a case home. You can't disregard anything because you never know what will pan out."

"Good. I'm glad I could help."

"What sort of work do you do here, Mrs. Wolfe?"

"Marybeth," she corrected him. "I'm a systems analyst. My job is to help integrate the software programs used by various departments so they can communicate with one another through their computers. It would be like the accounting department talking French and the marketing department talking German."

"Sounds interesting."

She laughed. "It has its moments."

Barnett smiled. "Just out of curiosity, what was your impression of Dr. Gumpta? Were you pleased with how he handled your case?"

She looked surprised. "Didn't he tell you?"

Barnett acted deadpan. "No. Patient confidentiality and all that. He just gave me your name."

She frowned. "I didn't like his attitude. He's one of those doctors who thinks they're God. Think they know everything. Nobody knows everything. Not even doctors."

"How so?"

"He wouldn't accept me as a patient."

"Why not?"

She stared at Barnett, her blue eyes large, perfect. "That's exactly what I wanted to know."

Chapter 39

An officer had been immediately dispatched to Ann Sleser's apartment as soon as Caggiano learned where she lived. The address that Barnett gave him over the phone from Dr. Gumpta's office was an old one, and she hadn't yet informed Motor Vehicles of the change. Caggiano had to visit her former apartment, learn from a neighbor that she worked as a cook in a downtown restaurant, then go there to obtain her current address. The restaurant, unfortunately, didn't open until three o'clock.

Around three-thirty, the officer radioed headquarters and reported that the apartment was locked and nobody answered his repeated knocks. Caggiano gave him strict instructions that no one was to enter until he, Barnett, or Quill arrived.

Quill was finishing up a drug-related homicide in Northwest when he got the call to meet Caggiano and Barnett at Sleser's apartment in Cleveland Park.

Using a key from the resident manager, Barnett opened the door.

Standing in the hallway, the three men craned their necks to see inside. The place was extraordinarily neat and clean. Not a scrap of paper was out of place.

211

"Did anyone even live here?" said Quill as he reached into his case for the camera. Caggiano and Barnett watched as Quill took pictures of the door, the jamb, and moved inside cautiously over the wooden floor.

Caggiano turned to Barnett who was still eyeing Quill's foray into the room. "It didn't happen here," he said. "This place looks like a museum."

Barnett was about to turn his head to Caggiano when something caught his attention. "Stop!" he screamed. Quill froze in mid-step, his left foot hanging in air.

"Look." He pointed about six inches in front of Quill's dangling foot.

Quill put his left foot down next to his right and squatted. "Faint. A man's shoe judging from the size." He took closeups of the footprint. "There's another," he said, pointing about eighteen inches away. "It's better defined."

"Can we lift it?" said Barnett from the hallway.

"We better. The pictures aren't going to be good enough. There's no contrast." He backed out, stepping only where he had walked before.

"I'll call in for the dust print lifter. It's not something I carry around. In fact, I've only used it once." Quill borrowed the portable radio from the officer and contacted his office. A voice said it would take thirty minutes.

"Good eye," said Caggiano. "I would've bet she wasn't taken from here. Everything's so immaculate."

"I'm still not sure, but I think Ann Sleser was such a neat freak that she would've cleaned that mark if she could have." Barnett and Caggiano walked the hallway. Barnett lowered his voice. "If we can establish that she was abducted from her apartment,

212

there's a chance the neighbors might have seen something."

"Drugs?"

"Had to be. We know that he used them on her for the videotape, and there's absolutely no sign of a struggle here."

"No forced entry either. The choices are always the same, Cag. She knew the killer, or she let in someone who people normally let in without fear."

Barnett took out his notebook and wrote the apartment numbers in order. He tore the page in half and handed it to Caggiano. "It'll give us something to do while we're waiting for Quill's gizmo." They walked in opposite directions.

Quill closed the apartment door, went down to his car, and read a magazine.

About an hour later, a mobile crime cruiser pulled up next to him. The driver shouted: "Hey, Quill. I got your print lifter."

Quill looked up. "It's about time. I could've gotten it myself. Stop along the way for a beer, Sandy?"

"Don't get on my case. I couldn't find the damn thing. Nobody knew where it was, let alone *what* it was."

"Figures."

"Anybody ever use it before?"

Quill stepped out of his car and approached Sandy Collins, the newest member of Mobile Crime. "I have." He took the attaché case. "You know, we buy all this good shit, and nobody ever uses it. All they know is fingerprints, fingerprints. Blow the powder, blow the powder. Fucking barbarians."

"Who's it for?"

"Barnett."

Collins showed interest. "Oh, yeah." He got out of his car and watched as Quill placed the case on the

213

car hood and checked the contents. Collins was dressed in a dark blue utility uniform and baseball cap. "Can I watch?" he asked.

"I don't see why not. Maybe you'll want to use it someday."

Caggiano and Barnett were disappointed that only three of the nine tenants on the floor were home. Caggiano talked to a retired bus driver who hadn't noticed anything unusual, but emphasized that he only looked out the window during commercials and rarely stepped outside except to go food shopping.

Barnett spoke to a college student who had been studying for days and wouldn't have heard anything short of fireworks over his walkman. The other person he interviewed, a mousy woman of ninety-two, said she was in bed all week with the flu.

All of them agreed, however, that the dead woman was rather shy and quiet until several months ago when she started saying hello and even became chatty.

"New boobs," said Barnett.

"What?"

"The implants. Flat-chested women are often introverted. Women have this thing about breasts that you and I will never understand." He thought about Marybeth Wolfe's visit to Dr. Gumpta and her unhappiness with her ample form.

"Did I hear something about breasts?" Quill said as he and Collins reached the door.

"I said hope springs eternal in the human breast, and I hope you can get me some good-looking prints," Barnett said, winking at Caggiano.

"This is Collins. He brought the unit and wants to see it work. Okay with you?"

Both Caggiano and Barnett nodded as Quill opened the door and stepped in cautiously. He got on his hands and knees in front of the first shoe print and opened the attaché case next to him.

Like a bomb specialist, Quill worked slowly and deliberately. He opened a cardboard mailing tube and removed a thin sheet of plastic. One side was black; the other side was silver. He hovered it a few inches above the print and handed it to Collins. "Take the scissors and cut it where my fingers are."

He took the cut sheet and put it on the floor next to the print. "Turn the lights off." He then got down with his face almost to the floor and beamed a flashlight over the black side. "You have to make sure there's not a speck of dust." He wiped a few particles away with a rag. Collins turned the lights back on.

Quill gently placed the sheet, black side down, over the shoe print. He took out the high-voltage power supply unit, a metal box with several knobs and wires sticking out.

One wire had connected to it what looked like a telescoping car antenna. Quill placed it about a half-inch away from the sheet and parallel to it. The other wire was attached to a thick insulated red probe. "Okay Collins, plug it in the wall."

Quill pressed a button, and the red light on the power supply lit. He twisted the voltage knob to mid-range and turned to Collins as Barnett and Caggiano watched attentively. "This will produce ten to fifteen kilovolts, but you don't have to worry about getting electrocuted because the amperage is very low."

He touched the tip of the high voltage probe to the edge of the sheet. Air bubbles in the sheet magically began to sink towards the floor. "It's going a little slower than it should be," he said as he turned up the voltage knob. The sheet sank further. When it was evenly pressed on the floor, Quill worked a rubber roller over it. He talked as he rolled.

"The electricity goes through the metal antenna, through the floor surface, through the sheet, and back to the probe. The dust particles are the same charge as the floor and are attracted to the sheet which has an opposite charge. That's why the sheet is attracted to the floor."

Quill turned off the power supply, waited about twenty seconds, and carefully peeled the sheet from the floor. When he turned it over, the men saw a perfectly formed shoe print down to the cuts and imperfections in the sole and heel. "Hit the lights again, Collins."

Quill took the sheet and held it at eye level. He motioned for Barnett to run the flashlight over it. "A low angle helps you see it better. That's it. What do you think, Mike?"

"Incredible."

Quill unfolded a cardboard carrying box which had been stored flat in the attaché case. He labeled the sheet, taped it to a thick piece of cardboard, and slid it vertically in the box so nothing touched it except the grooves at the edges.

"Ready for number two?" he said.

Quill spent the next twenty minutes lifting the second shoe print.

"It's even better than the first," said Barnett as he ran the flashlight over the sheet.

Quill gave Barnett a sideways glance. "How important is it that this be the killer's shoe print?"

"What are you saying, Joe?"

"The shoes found in the van were loafers. The soles had no designs. Just smooth leather. These prints are from brogans or some other kind of work shoe. The soles have nonskid type designs."

"Our man doesn't fit the profile of a brogan wearer, that's for sure," said Barnett.

He thought for a minute. "Remember that Cinderella Analysis thing I showed you several months ago in that forensic newsletter?"

"Vaguely. It didn't pass Frye if I recall."

"Right, but it's good enough for us. Want to give it a try?"

"Why not? My pumpkin doesn't come 'til midnight."

Chapter 40

"This is great, Quill," Barnett said. "It's like real cutting-edge cop stuff."

"Shut up and hand me the X-acto knife."

In Quill's office, the two were staring at a pair of loafers found in the van stolen from the fish market. Barnett handed Quill the razor knife kit.

"You know," Quill said as he loaded a fresh blade, "you haven't linked the van to the killer for certain. We're just guessing. Hand me the shoe."

"Right."

"No."

"No?"

"The left. Give me the friggin' left shoe."

"Oh. Here."

Quill began cutting the upper part of the shoe, slowly making his way around just above the stitching. About halfway he stopped to change blades. "Kills the edge. Weren't made to cut leather."

"I think the killer dressed himself as a fish worker—smock, hard hat, rubber boots. The whole outfit. He changed from street shoes to boots in the van."

Quill continued cutting. "And the water in the back of the van?"

"That was from Henkel. How or why he was wet I don't know. Maybe he fell on the sidewalk. The streets are always soaked from melted ice."

"Sounds plausible, but then again, I'm not the assistant DA. There," he pronounced, "one cut shoe."

Quill took the exposed shoe over to a large table next to the sheet with the shoe print. He placed them side by side. Barnett spoke. "According to the theory, the impression the foot makes on the inside of the shoe is directly responsible for the wear patterns on the outside of the sole and heel."

"Even if it's a different shoe?"

"Yep. Even if it's a different shoe." Barnett pulled a sheath of papers from his pocket and began to read. "We have to measure the total length, width across the ball, arch and heel. If you see any other wear patterns, we'll try to compare them, too."

Quill rifled his desk drawer, pushing aside debris. "What's the Frye deal again? It didn't pass, did it?" He continued his search at another set of desk drawers.

"No. An anthropologist named Louise Robbins at the University of North Carolina had been doing some work on imprints. She testified at a murder trial in Illinois that shoe prints found at the scene compared with shoes found at the home of the prime suspect. Robbins determined that the shoes, which made the imprints at the scene, and boots found at the suspect's home were worn by the same person."

"And the jury bought it?"

"Yes. Even though she said under cross-examination that she had never taken a course in shoe identification and that she didn't know of any studies in the U.S. similar to hers. She could name four people overseas who were working in the field, but that was it."

Quill finally found the metal rule for which he was looking.

"She must have made a compelling argument because they found the guy guilty. It was overturned on appeal when the court said her procedure hadn't gained general acceptance in the scientific community."

"Legally, that's true, but it sounds right to me," Quill said, sitting down again at the table.

"Me, too. It makes sense."

"Okay, let's see what we got." Quill took measurements, starting with the inside of the shoe, calling them out to Barnett who recorded them on a chart labeled "left shoe." After taking about eight measurements, he turned to the print on the black sheet. "Unfortunately, we can't get any depth measurements like we could from an impression, but at least we can note some of the obvious high and low points."

Making certain not to touch the print itself, Quill held the rule over the sheet and called out numbers to Barnett who had already drawn a chart called "left print."

Barnett studied the numbers. "Geeze. It's pretty close. Look," he said, holding the paper so Quill could see it.

"I'll be damned," said Quill. "Let's do the other shoe."

They repeated the process and again held the two charts next to each other. "Amazing," said Quill.

Barnett called Caggiano on the phone. "Quill and

I did that Cinderella thing and I'll tell you something, it looked pretty good to me. I'm willing to bet that Sleser was taken from her apartment. I think we should heavily canvass the building tonight when everyone's home."

"I'll give you a hand."

"Good. We need to give them a window."

"The restaurant said she didn't come into work on Wednesday. Her day off is Tuesday, and they're closed on Sundays and Mondays. She leaves work at midnight."

"That gives us Saturday after midnight to . . . when did the tape arrive at the station?"

"Wednesday."

"Okay. Saturday after midnight 'til let's say Tuesday afternoon to allow for next day mailing time."

"The ME said she died within seventy-two hours but that doesn't really help. We know when she was killed, but not when she was snatched. Let's check her mailbox and answering machine and see if we can narrow it a little."

"About eight?"

"Sounds good," Barnett said. "Can you pick me up at my place?"

"I'll be there."

When they arrived at Sleser's apartment building, Barnett jumped out first. He pushed the button for the resident manager and was buzzed in. Caggiano was right behind.

They looked over the bank of mailboxes and found Sleser's. Through the cutout design in the door, they could see envelopes and magazines jammed together. Barnett reached into his back pocket and produced a small leather case. He looked at Caggiano. "Don't ask."

Caggiano stood silent.

From among the choice of probes, straight, curved, crooked, and angled Barnett lifted a piece that resembled a skeleton key. It fit perfectly into the mailbox drawer above the individual boxes. It opened down, like a door transom, and Barnett reached his arm down into Sleser's box and began plucking out mail and handing it to Caggiano. When the box was bare, he closed and locked the drawer.

"Okay, okay. I had a pal who was a mailman. He gave me the key. It comes in handy. Saves time."

"Did I ask?" said Caggiano as he nonchalantly leafed through the mail.

They took the elevator up.

"Based on the postmarks of the local stuff, I'd say she picked up her mail on Saturday after work, but not on Monday," Caggiano said.

Barnett sounded afraid. "Anything from—"

"No. Bills and junk mail."

They peeled off the Crime Scene tape and entered the immaculate apartment. Over by an end table, the light was still blinking on the answering machine. They had decided before, when they examined the room and took the shoe print, to leave the machine alone. Although it was becoming accepted homicide procedure to take phone machines from a crime scene, Barnett had discovered recently that some newer models sometimes didn't play back messages properly if the power was cut. If the owner didn't rewind the messages once they were listened to, a stranger could mistake it for a recent one instead of a message from last week that had already been retrieved.

This was the case with Sleser's machine. The message counter said two messages were waiting, but after listening to them, Barnett also heard three messages preceding it on the tape.

"How'd you ever get so smart?" said Caggiano.

"Been hanging out with Quill."

From the contents of the messages, Barnett decided Sleser had last listened to them on Sunday night. "I think we're pretty safe asking the neighbors about Monday and Tuesday."

"Let's do it." Barnett again made up a list of apartments and the two headed in opposite directions.

An hour later in the car, they compared notes.

"Everyone," said Barnett.

"Same. What did you get?"

"Two things," said Barnett. "I got a Federal Express guy Monday about nine and an exterminator around noon. Resident manager said it's the same exterminator they've been using for twenty years and the Fed Ex guy was Hispanic. Erase them both."

Caggiano thumbed his notepad. "I have a mailman around dusk. Man who lives in the front said he was looking out the window. The mailman pulled up in his car, double-parked, and ran inside the building. He didn't see him come out. When he looked out the window about a half-hour later, the car was gone."

"Did he describe the mailman?"

"White. Thirties."

"Cag. I'm not a prejudiced man, am I?" he said with a smile. "But how many white mailmen are there in the District of Columbia?"

"Possible," said Caggiano. "Is there any way to check with the Post Office about whether one of their people came by here that day?"

Barnett shot Caggiano a look and they both laughed. "Yeah, right."

"Okay, you can buy the uniform. It's easy to get those, but the car?"

"Why not? Let's see if there are any listed as stolen."

"If not?"

"Hell. All it would take is the purchase of a Pinto and a paint job. Bet you can buy one of those Nader firebombs cheap," Barnett said.

"That's probably why the government has them."

"This guy's a perfectionist. He'd want to do things right. I can see him dressing up as a mailman with the car and everything. I think he dressed up as a fish worker. This would be right up his alley. It would sure explain how he got in the building and in her apartment without a struggle. It would also explain the work shoes. That's not our guy's style. He's more of a Gucci wing tip man, but he would have to go for the complete mailman look."

Caggiano thought for a minute. "Probably wouldn't be the first time for the mailman trick."

"Albert DeSalvo," said Barnett.

Caggiano looked puzzled.

"The Boston strangler. He used it."

They talked about how they'd have to check all the uniform stores in the area as well as used-car dealers and paint shops—assuming the Post Office wasn't already shy a vehicle.

Caggiano eased the car in front of Barnett's home. "Want to come in for a beer, Cag? It's still early."

"No, thanks."

"Going out?"

"Yes."

"Will I ever meet this mysterious lady friend, Cag?" Barnett said, opening the door.

"Perhaps. If you're lucky."

"I'll cross my fingers." He closed the car door and walked to his front door, picking up one of Penny's toys along the way.

"Maybe we can double date, Mike," Caggiano said to himself as he peeled away. "That would be a great match. Your wife and my . . . lady friend."

Chapter 41

Caggiano parked his car at Logan Circle and strolled up and down the block looking for Damian. He made several passes but hadn't spotted her in all the usual places. He glanced inside the 7-11, cupping his face against the glare of the plate-glass window. Sometimes she talked with the night clerk, a Lebanese college student who gave Damian free coffee in exchange for leering privileges. He didn't see her.

Since his wife had left him, Caggiano found solace in women of the night. He had tried several others, but none had Damian's gentleness. A warmth that went through him. A caring that seemed real even though Caggiano knew it wasn't. He had admitted to himself a long time ago that Damian was, after all, a whore who went with whomever came up with the right price first.

Still, he was jealous of her suitors. Down deep he felt a special affection for her and always thought, against his intellectual self, that she felt something special for him as well.

He knew he was being silly feeling this way about her, but he couldn't help himself. He craved a woman's touch, even if he had to pay for it. Go out

227

with straight women? He had. His friends had fixed him up, but it didn't work, and he didn't know why. Maybe it was cleaner to pay for it. No complications. No demands. It was hard to start a new love life.

Caggiano wanted desperately to talk to Damian about their last meeting at the Tabard Inn, the only time she really needed him to stay the night. What was that all about? Was something changing in their relationship? He wanted to see her even more now that he replayed the night in his head.

As Caggiano looked down the block he thought he saw Damian's silhouette. He couldn't call to her. Too far away. The whole neighborhood would hear. He walked quickly in her direction.

He saw her thin body throw a sharp shadow against the sidewalk. It was her. He was sure of it.

"Damian," he screamed but stifled it before the second syllable left his mouth. Did she turn towards him? Did she see him?

No.

Caggiano stepped up his pace.

His heart beat faster.

"Damian," he said under his breath.

Just as he arrived, the shadow vanished inside a car.

Caggiano watched the car pull away. The figure in the driver's seat wore a cowboy hat, the other person was tying back her hair.

As they sped up fourteenth street, the silhouette in the passenger side leaned over towards the driver and disappeared.

Caggiano closed his eyes, took a deep breath, and beat the fleshy part of his fist against the building's brick wall.

He knew it wouldn't do any good to cry, but he did anyway.

Chapter 42

Barnett was sitting at his desk in front of three opened Yellow Pages books when Caggiano walked in, his eyes red, his gait uncharacteristically slow.

"Rough night?" Barnett said, smiling.

Caggiano didn't hear him and went into his office. Barnett followed.

"You okay, Cag?"

"Yeah, fine. Just had a late night. I'm okay. Really."

Barnett began to say something then stopped. Caggiano rubbed his eyes. "What do you have?"

"I called the Postal Inspector's office first thing. As far as they're concerned, all vehicles are accounted for. The person I spoke with," he checked his notebook, "Agent Charles Kerrigan, said postal service offices around the country are seeing an increase in, and I quote, 'unauthorized and illegal uniform activity.'"

"I love fedtalk."

"I thought you would. From what Kerrigan says, more than a few wiseguys are using postal uniforms to gain access to office buildings. Purse lifting and stuff. Nothing violent. If we've got an, ahem, illegal uniform activity, he said he wanted to know about it. I told him we weren't sure but would keep him posted."

"Has he ever come across a phony mail car?"

"That was a new one on him. He couldn't understand why somebody would want to go through all that trouble when just the uniform would do. I didn't go into detail."

Caggiano poured a cup of coffee and downed it like a whiskey shot.

Barnett continued. "He gave me a list of stores in the area that carry postal uniforms, but he also said his list was a year old and to check the phone directories for new stores. There's about two dozen. He also said there's some mail-order shops, but I doubt our man would use them."

"Checks and credit cards only."

"Of course. I also asked Auto for a list of possible sources for a Pinto along with paint shops."

"Big list?"

"Not as big as you'd think. They suggested we first try junk dealers who buy from federal auctions. Believe it or not, Auto offered us two people. It must be my charm," Barnett said.

"And an early morning call from Wilson. He's trying to be a nice guy."

"Just by staying out of my face is nice enough for me."

When Barnett stopped talking, the room turned suddenly very quiet. Even the noise from outside the office didn't intrude. Barnett sat down. "What's going on, Cag?"

He tried to be cheery. "Woman trouble. You know."

"Anything I can do?"

"We've got to work it out ourselves."

"The offer stands. Carol and I would love to have you guys over. Just say when."

"Thanks. I'll let you know."

"What are you doing for the next few days. Want to check out some auto shops?"

Caggiano looked at all the papers on his desk. "I really shouldn't, but you know I will. Let's see those lists."

"I'll call Auto, have them meet us downstairs. We'll divvy it up," said Barnett.

Caggiano walked to the copy machine, made several copies and reached Barnett's desk just as he got off the phone. "I figure two, maybe three days with four of us working," Caggiano said.

"How about you and I take the uniforms and Auto takes the rest."

Caggiano nodded.

In the parking lot, Caggiano and Barnett met Simpson and Kirk. The two had been in Auto for three years, despising every minute, and they told anyone who came their way about it.

Barnett didn't bother with the usual "how's it going?" knowing full well it would just be an opportunity for them to complain. Auto had lately been used as a dumping ground for detectives who got uppity or otherwise displeased their superiors.

Barnett knew Simpson and Kirk when they were in Vice and came upon a drug dealer who supplied a member of the mayor's inner circle with high-grade cocaine. Without warning, the two found themselves transferred to Auto over the protests of their FOP representative. They were more angry at the lack of confidence their superiors had in them than anything else. "All they had to do was say the word. We would've laid off," Simpson had told everyone around him. Kirk was even more vocal. He had a wife and three kids and the extra money made in Vice was sorely missed. "Can't make any dough in Auto" became his daily gripe.

Both were still hoping to make it back into Vice before their twenty was up. That could have been why Barnett found them surprisingly friendly and eager to help.

Kirk, the younger of the two, wore boots, fresh jeans, a dark shirt, and a sweater. He took the list from Barnett and said, "Know all these guys. They're our pals. No sweat."

Simpson wore a blue suit, white shirt, and yellow tie. "No problem at all, Barnett," he said, looking over the list. "Phony car's always a good hustle. Had a case several months ago where a guy painted a van with the Domino's Pizza logo. Had the orange and blue jacket, too. He got in more fuckin' places then you'd believe. Even people who didn't order pizza let him in their homes. He went for women, robbed, beat, and raped them. Then you know what he did? He called for a pizza delivery. The neighborhood was getting freaked, and it was getting so bad the Domino's drivers were afraid to deliver to this one area in Mount Pleasant where he hit three houses, bam, bam, bam, right in a row. One night a woman answered the door and panicked when she saw a delivery boy. She shot him with a tear gas pen right in the face 'cause she didn't like the way he looked at her." Simpson laughed. "And she'd called for a large pepperoni and onion."

Chapter 43

"How was your talk with Detective Barnett?"

"Exhilarating. A great mind. He's quite good-looking, too."

"So, you're taken with him then?"

"Taken's not the right word, darling, but I am attracted to him in a certain way. It's a challenge. You know what I mean, don't you?"

"I do. I chose him because he's the best. Not to mention his domestic situation. Do you think he'll go any further?"

"There's really no reason to. He gave me some song and dance about checking out the other connections to Ann, but he was just humoring me, trying not to hurt my feelings. I was so earnest about giving him . . ." She affected a Southern accent. "What do you policemen call it . . . a lead?" Marybeth laughed.

"You should have been an actress, darling," Harlan Wolfe said as he put his arm around her waist and pulled her close.

They kissed.

Marybeth arched her neck back, touched a finger to his lips. "How does it make you feel that we've talked

233

to Detective Barnett and his wife and neither of them suspect anything about us?"

"I kind of like it. It's, as you say, exhilarating."

"Is it everything you thought it would be?"

Wolfe thought for a minute before answering. "So far it's been grand, but there's still something missing. It lacks that final thrust, a . . . denouement."

"Oh, Harlan. I love when you talk French to me." They both laughed as Marybeth glided to the wet bar and poured champagne from a half-empty bottle. "A refill?"

He nodded.

Marybeth walked back to the couch, collapsed her legs underneath her body on the rug in front of Harlan. Her robe was opened, exposing a black teddy. She handed him a glass and placed her head in his lap. He stroked her hair.

"Harlan," she said, staring into space. "Do you think he knows what we're all about? Do you think he understands?"

"I don't think anyone understands but us. How could they? Nobody knows what we've been through, what we've endured, what we've seen." His voice had an edge.

She picked her head up, looked in his eyes. "Oh, Harlan," she said in a baby voice. "You don't think they ever will? Ever, ever." She began to cry then looked away.

"Marybeth, I—"

Suddenly, she bolted upright and pounced like a cat. He tried to protect himself by crossing his hands in front of his face, but they flared out when she tickled him. The glass went flying. "Ha!" she shouted, "gotcha!"

"You bitch!"

"Gotcha, gotcha!" She continued tickling him

until he begged her to stop.

Finally, they nestled together on the couch. She opened his shirt, toyed with his chest hairs.

"Do you think he enjoyed our video production?" she asked.

"I suspect he's seen it tens of times, probably showed it to a few shrinks."

"He's pretty smart. He might just understand."

His voice became sincere. "We were kidding about it before, but this is serious." He held her face in his hands. "Nobody understands us, MB. Nobody."

She buried her face in his neck. "Nobody," she whispered.

Chapter 44

Barnett wasn't all that hopeful that checking used-car dealers for recent Pinto sales and uniform stores would be of any help. He was sure the killer would have paid cash. After all he'd done, there was no way he would slip up on something as simple as leaving a credit-card trail. Still, procedure called for him to track down any leads, no matter how weak. Besides, Barnett had always believed in the "You Never Know" theory and the corollary that said, "Keep Busy."

After two days of riding around the District and suburbs, Barnett, Caggiano, Kirk, and Simpson met at the Dubliner to discuss their findings. Barnett was surprised to see how much territory each of them had covered.

Kirk took a sip of Guinness and began. "About six months ago, a white male, thirties, good-looking, bought an orange Seventy-Nine Pinto from a dealer in Arlington." He looked up at Barnett. "It's one of those ancient wooden houses with used cars on the front lawn. Christmas lights strung all year round. Usually in the middle of the high rises or a neighborhood on the edge of a commercial area. Know the kind I mean?"

Barnett nodded. "I've always wondered about them. They don't seem to do any business."

"Selling cars are almost an afterthought. Usually, the owner has the house and land paid for, and he sells cars to keep his property actively zoned commercial so he can sell it to a developer. If he stopped using it for business, the neighbors might try to rezone it for residential only." He took another sip and continued. "These places are also money-laundering banks for the mob."

"Or bookie joints," said Simpson.

"That, too," said Kirk. "Anyway, there's a guy on Columbia Pike, Bob's Used Cars, sold the Pinto to a man who fits your profile. He remembered the guy because he didn't seem like the Pinto type. He pulled up in a green Jag and paid cash. Seven-hundred-fifty dollars. Saw him coming."

Barnett looked at Caggiano. "That's it, Cag. The big green car we've been dancing around. It's a Jaguar."

"That's important to you?" said Kirk.

"Sure is," said Barnett.

"Then don't forget where you heard it," Kirk said seriously.

"Don't forget," Simpson repeated.

"We won't. Anything else? What about the paint job?"

"I checked on that," said Simpson. "Nobody remembers an orange Pinto at any of the legitimate shops. I even checked a couple of underground boys and came up zero. My guess is that he took a couple of gallons of white gloss and painted it himself. But," he emphasized, "I went a little further. You said he was a perfectionist, likes to get things right. I checked with a couple of pinstriping places and two of them got a call from someone who wanted to put red and blue pinstripes on a white Pinto. The caller said he was in the movie business and needed the car for a film. The owners said to come by, but he never did."

Barnett was about to speak but was interrupted. "Then I checked some over-the-counter pinstriping places and came up with a store on Georgia Avenue by the Maryland line that sold a blue and red pinstriping kit to a white man in his thirties. The counterman recalled him because he wanted some decal numbers and—"

"The vehicle numbers on the back," said Barnett, thinking aloud.

"Right. And he also wanted to know where he could get a postal insignia, the one with the eagle, for the side. Same story, said he was making a movie. The counterman sold him the pinstriping and numbers but said he didn't know where to get the eagle insignia except from the company that made them for the Postal Service."

Kirk chimed in. "I can tell you how he got the insignia, Barnett. It's easier than you think." Simpson lowered his head, nodded, as if to say, "This is old stuff."

"All you do is take a photo of a real insignia, enlarge it, and paste it on the car. In fact, last year Simpson and I served a warrant on a boyo in Gaithersburg who a snitch said was selling phony DC inspection stickers. When we searched his garage we found a complete color negative file with federal vehicle insignias, but we couldn't get him on anything other than selling the stickers. It turns out they were real. He had a compadre at the Mount Olivet inspection station who ripped off a couple of boxes."

"His pal would send the failures to him and they would fix the driver up for fifty bucks. Then another guy would play the Motor Vehicle computer until it

239

changed its tune to pass instead of fail," said Simpson. "It was a nice little operation."

Kirk continued: "We called the Secret Service, thinking it was against counterfeiting laws to possess the insignias. They came and took a look and pronounced it kosher after the man said he collected the photos as a hobby."

"What happened to them?" said Caggiano.

"The guy in Gaithersburg walked when he turned in his buddy at the inspection station. That guy, in turn, rolled over on his buddy who worked the computer. They both lost their jobs. One of them works at a gas station in Maryland; the other one, the inspector, does brake jobs for Midas in Virginia."

"Is your man in Gaithersburg still in business?" asked Barnett.

"We checked," said Kirk. "He won three-quarter mil in the Maryland lottery. He doesn't do shit anymore. Sits around."

"See? And people say there is no God," said Simpson, laughing. "Just out of curiosity, how'd you do on the uniforms?"

"I got a white male, thirties, buying a postal uniform about six months ago," said Caggiano. "Paid cash. In fact, that's why the salesman remembered him. First of all, he was white." He glanced over at Barnett, who smiled. "And he paid cash. All, and I mean all, legitimate postal workers pay by check or credit card, because they take the uniforms off their taxes and need the proof of purchase. He distinctly remembers the man asking for the 'letter carrier' patch, too. It was our guy. The profile fits perfectly and we got a new piece. Red hair."

"Cute," said Barnett. "Red-haired people marry each other." He looked at Kirk's puzzled face. "We also have a woman with red hair who figures in this.

240

We'll need you guys a little longer, okay?"

"Anything," said Simpson, "anything."

"Check your records for a green Jaguar, owner is male or female or both, white, twenty-five to forty, both with red hair. Can you do it?"

"Of course," said Kirk, "but it may take a while. The program we have is old and slow. I'd also guess it'll kick out quite a few possibles."

"We're glad to do anything we can for you and Caggiano," said Simpson.

"Boys," Barnett said, smiling, raising his glass, "you're going to make me lose my beer."

"To lost beer," said Simpson.

"And newly found assignments," said Kirk.

Chapter 45

The number that appeared on Barnett's pager seemed familiar, but he couldn't place it, so he didn't return the call immediately. Instead, he continued reading for the fifth time the jacket on Ann Sleser. When he was through, he sat in deep thought.

The pager warbled again. The same number. Barnett finally dialed.

"It's about time you called."

"Quill? I thought today's your day off. Why aren't you out cruising the Beltway holding an ace in the hole? Willy throw you out?"

"Listen, Barnett, I got something to show you. Come out to my place."

Barnett had known Quill for almost ten years and had been to his house only twice. Once to carry him home drunk from a bachelor party when he himself passed out on the couch. The other time he brought Quill a paycheck while he was recovering from an appendectomy.

"To what do I owe this honor?"

"Honor my ass. Get yourself out here. I'm gonna make your day. Maybe your year."

"What's it got to do with—" The phone went dead.

"Crazy nut," Barnett whispered to himself and headed out.

Quill lived in a working-class neighborhood called Del Ray, a vibrant railroad town from the turn of the century until the 1920's when it was annexed by the city of Alexandria, losing its original name of Potomac.

With rail traffic all but gone, developers were planning to convert the massive unused yards into a continuation of Crystal City along Jefferson Davis Highway.

The rail yards hid the area from outsiders, especially those who could no longer afford to live in tony Old Town a mile away and were searching for affordable housing in a real neighborhood.

Already, emigrants from Old Town were descending upon Del Ray on top of the working-class whites, blacks, and hispanics, raising property values and taxes. Like others in Del Ray, Quill wanted the world to stay out.

Quill's house had been built for railroad shift workers and had three separate bedrooms on the second floor, an attic, dining and living rooms, and a basement. The porch had a hammock surrounded by potted plants. His garden was lush.

Barnett always thought the house was too big for a bachelor. Like Quill, it was neat, unpretentious, and comfortable.

Quill answered the door, wearing brown chino pants and a sweatshirt. "What took you so long?" he said, waving a beer in Barnett's face. He walked to the kitchen, tossing the bottle in the trash can and opening the refrigerator. "Want one?"

"I'll take one," Barnett said.

"Downstairs," Quill commanded.

Barnett followed him down cement stairs. Quill

held a shirt drying on a line to the side so Barnett could pass without getting wet.

Barnett knew Quill was a tinkerer, but what he saw took him aback. "Where'd you get all this?"

"Got a friend in Property. He lent me all the cameras except that JVC at the end. It's mine."

Barnett counted ten video cameras and camcorders stacked on a workbench along with some other gear he recognized by their logos: an Apple computer, Hewlett-Packard laser printer, and a Tektronix oscilloscope.

Quill took a pull on his beer and watched Barnett absorb what he saw. "I guess you're wondering what all this is, huh, Mike?"

"No, Quill. Hadn't occurred to me to ask."

"Okay, I'll tell you. You've known me for what . . . ten years? What is it that I've always wanted to do?"

"Have sex with Rosemary in Records."

"Besides that."

"I don't know, Quill." Barnett scanned the rat's nest of wires. "Make an atom bomb? I don't know."

"Close. I've always wanted to have something published in a scholarly magazine, you know, like the *Journal of Forensic Sciences.*" He stood in front of the bench and turned around to Barnett. "I've been working on this for about a year, and I'm almost ready to publish my work."

Quill walked over to a file cabinet. "I wouldn't show this to anybody else in the office but you. I know you'll appreciate it. Not like the others."

Barnett shot him a funny look, and Quill laughed.

"That sounds kind of Frankensteinish, doesn't it? Let me rephrase that. A lot of guys make fun of people who want to get ahead, make some contribution beyond putting in their time. They're not interested in new equipment and techniques, but you and I love that stuff. It's a rush for us. It's fun."

"Keep talking."

"Remember the work the FBI did on photocopy machines? Where they could tell what kind of copier made which copy?

"They compiled a list of characteristics especially, what did they call them, trash marks? The little lines and scratches on the sides and bottom of the sheet. Each model copier has its own fingerprint.

"Not only that, but each individual machine leaves its own unique markings. Here." Quill produced a reprint titled: *The Classification of Office Copy Machines from Physical Characteristics*. "The FBI has a data base of seventeen-hundred models. If you get a photocopy you can check it against the data base. All you need is an Apple Computer and a search program." He walked back to the bench. "I'm trying to do the same thing with video cameras."

Barnett finished his beer and tossed the bottle in a metal can. "Nobody's doing it already?"

"Have you heard something I haven't? If the FBI's working on it, they aren't talking, but I got to believe they've been looking into it. They're getting too many videotapes not to pay attention."

Quill pressed some keys on the computer and continued talking. "I've been talking to a friend who's an electronics genius, and the concept's relatively simple. He helped me buy what I needed and sent me diagrams on how to hook it up. My physics degree doesn't hurt either."

Barnett stood fascinated. "Let's see it work."

"First let me explain what you'll see. Think of two cars starting. Each one has a unique sound during that interval between turning the key and actually running. If you had good enough ears, you could actually tell which car was which by the sound. In fact, you probably could easily tell the difference between a VW starting and a Maserati."

"While it's running, too."

"Absolutely. Now suppose we had two VWs, both the same model. You might not be able to tell which was which while it was running, but you might be able to distinguish them by the start-up sound. That's still unique to each engine because it's quite a complex procedure."

Barnett made a face. "Forget the cars. Tell me about the cameras."

"I need to work on that car analogy, don't I? Okay, what happens with cameras is that while they're running there's not much difference in what the resulting tape looks like under instrumentation. Just like photocopy machines, cameras leave electronic trash marks on the tape. The only problem with using them for identification is that there aren't enough marks or indicators to look at. Just like the car running as opposed to starting. However, there's more happening, more to look at, when they're starting and stopping than when they're running. So what I've decided to do is look at the start-up and shutdown sequence of the machines."

"You mean when you push the start and stop buttons?"

"Yes. That very short sequence is unique to each model." He pointed to an oscilloscope screen with a wavy line. "This is the start-up sequence of the color burst oscillator of my camcorder. Don't ask me to explain what a color burst oscillator is. Just trust me that it's the gizmo that starts putting color on your TV picture when you turn it on. If you look at the wave it makes over a fifty to sixty microsecond interval you see this jitter pattern."

Barnett put his finger on the screen. "This is frozen in time?"

"Yes. I can hold the image for as long as I want even after it's gone. In the twenty or so models that I've looked at each has a different jitter pattern. So much so that I could tell which pattern came from which machine. Each pattern is a function of the physical components like the motor and the electronic components like the chips. Now we take it another step." Quill pointed to the computer screen filled with random numbers.

"You take that jitter pattern and sample it, meaning you break it up into smaller and smaller pieces until you're left with a connection of dots. Each dot is assigned a number based on how far it is from the bottom line, kind of like a ruler, and then you put all the numbers into the computer. It uses something called digital-signal processing. It's similar to voice-recognition devices where you take something that's analog, your voice, convert it into something digital, numbers, and display it."

"Where'd you get this?"

"Bought it by mail. Five hundred bucks. The technology's scary, isn't it?"

"Then what?"

"So basically, I've got the start-up chacteristics of one camera displayed on the screen with numbers. Then I do the same thing for another camera."

"And compare the two."

"Correct. You use software called a pattern recognition program to compare the thousands of numbers from each machine. It's more accurate than trying to compare the wave patterns on the screen by eye. It also allows you an easy way to store the information because it's just numbers."

"How accurate is it?"

"Very, but it depends upon how small a sample you take. The smaller the interval you look at, the more accurate you'll be. What I've found is that by taking a smaller and smaller interval you can eventually tell which machine, not just which model, you're looking at. That's been the bulk of my work, finding that perfect time interval big enough to contain useful information yet small enough for that information to be unique."

"And no one else is working on this?"

"I'm not breaking totally new ground. The military has been working on pattern recognition for years. They use it to distinguish between friendly and unfriendly radio transmissions like radar by looking at the very beginning and very end of a transmission. Transmitters exhibit unique start-up and shutdown characteristics, too. As far as cameras are concerned, I'm sure somebody's working on it, but nobody's published anything."

"We're starting to see videotapes coming our way. It would be nice to know where they're coming from."

"That's why I say I'm sure other people are working on it. I've got to believe that the CIA and FBI have tracked down the type of machine that made tapes of the Lebanon hostages. And Scotland Yard and M5 have got to be on top of this because of the tapes they get from the IRA."

"Maybe they've been doing it and not telling anyone?"

"That's what I think, but they're so damn paranoid about the bad guys knowing what they know that they won't give it to the people who could use it. Like us."

"Have you already checked the tape we got from the killer?"

"No, I didn't want to take it until I checked with the TV station to see if the one they gave us is the original and not a copy they made."

"And?"

"It's the original. Straight from the killer's camera."

Barnett described how he, Caggiano, and the two men from Auto didn't find any paper trails left by the killer when he bought his postal car and uniform. "If this guy's smart as I think he is, he paid cash for the camera too, knowing one day he might use it for something like this. But I'll tell you one thing I bet he couldn't resist doing."

Quill's eyes widened.

"I bet he filled out the warranty card and mailed it to the company. And that would have the make and model, wouldn't it?"

"Sure would. And most companies will give us the names any way we want it, including by zip code. I checked. Hell, they sell mailing lists to the video aftermarket."

"If your system works as well as—"

"It does."

"—you think, we may have something here." Barnett filled Quill in on the computer lists that Kirk and Simpson were working on. "When can you start?"

"Today. I'll ride back downtown with you and get the tape. If I get lucky, I'll already have the match on file, if not, I'll have to keep borrowing more cameras from the property division. You wouldn't believe how many they have there."

"Let's have another beer to celebrate. My treat. I'll trek to the refrigerator." As he walked upstairs his pager went off. This time he recognized the number as Monika Sidor's.

250

"Mike, I've been watching a copy of the tape we made and after seeing it again and again, I think you'd better be extra careful."

"I'm always careful."

"I'm serious. That incident was a turning point for him. That episode with Henkel was in itself traumatic, and the more I think about what I told you at the time, the more I think I was right. He's out looking for the perfect partner to finish his play. I can't tell you who it will be, but it's going to be someone heavy, like a female cop or a congresswoman, somebody with visibility and power. He's getting more anxious every day."

Quill walked upstairs to the kitchen. Barnett handed him a beer. "Thanks for the warning, Monny. I think we're getting close." He held the bottle up to Quill. "I've got an ace in the hole."

Chapter 46

For the first time in the investigation, Barnett felt strangely optimistic. There were still a lot of ifs, but if it clicked, the whole case would fall into place.

He had to believe it was his best shot. Because if Monny was right, and the killer was getting ready for some sort of grand finish, it would be his last shot, too.

Quill was working as fast as he could, but only at night and in his off hours. As for Auto, it might take a week for them to compile a list unless they could clear all other work.

Barnett hadn't seen Wilson since the post mortem on the failed fish market stakeout. As usual, they were avoiding each other.

"Think he'll go for it?" said Barnett as he and Caggiano walked towards the captain's office.

"Getting more out of Auto and Motor Vehicles is doable, but taking Quill off the job with all the drug homicides is not something he's going to like. He's always scared shitless that the media's going to find out about some unorthodox scheme that makes sense at the time but sounds stupid to outsiders. Quill's experiments are a chancy proposition. Not to mention that he likes and trusts Quill as much as he does you." Caggiano smiled. "But it can't hurt to ask, can it?"

Wilson was on the phone and he stared up and said, "May I call you back, sir. I've got an emergency." He took some time straightening papers and said, "You saved me the trouble of calling for you both. Sit."

Caggiano and Barnett sat at attention, puzzled looks on their faces.

"That was the chief. The mayor got a letter today from our killer. All it said was, 'Ready for the big finish? I am.' They're sending it over now. It contained a piece of wire."

"Monny was right," Barnett said under his breath.

"What?"

"Monika Sidor. She said the killer's getting ready for a grand finale. Take out somebody special, a policewoman or some politico. Someone with high visibility."

"Why wasn't I notified?"

"She just told me. Besides, what would you do, go on TV and tell important women not to leave their homes?"

"In case you don't know where we are, Detective Barnett, this is Washington, DC. We not only take care of our own residents but high visibility people who work here. If one of them is in danger I want to know about it. I shouldn't have to hear it from the chief. I read your reports, Barnett, and you haven't done jack shit. I haven't seen one indication that you're progressing. The chief wants me to take you off the case and I agree."

"You can't do that."

"Oh, no? Watch me. You're off the case. See? Caggiano, put someone else on it. How about Kelleher or Stein? Turn over all your notes to them."

"You know something, Captain? I used to think you were an asshole. I was wrong. You're a flaming asshole. Nobody can do a better job than me and you know it."

"Really? Show me. You're a cop. Let's see the evidence. Give me one good reason why I shouldn't take you off the case."

"Quill," said Barnett.

"What does that rummy have to do with it?"

"He's working on something that could break it wide open for us."

"What'd he do? Find out what kind of beer the killer likes and test all the samples?"

Barnett ignored the comment and explained the video project.

"You're just as crazy as he is," said Wilson. "If that procedure's for real, why isn't the FBI working on it?"

"They may be, but Quill hasn't been able to get them to tell him anything. Quill says it'll work, and I believe him."

Wilson thought for a minute. "Caggiano?"

"It's the best chance we have. Might be the only chance."

"One week. That's all. I'll tell the chief . . . I don't know . . . something. And don't forget, Barnett, I'm not doing this 'cause I believe in you. I believe in Caggiano. He wouldn't risk his career on something stupid, would he?" He turned from Barnett, held a mean glare on Caggiano, and grinned. Caggiano squinted his eyes.

"One more thing, Captain," said Barnett. "As long as we're pals, I have a favor to ask."

Wilson gritted his teeth.

"I want Quill taken off regular duty so he can work on this full time."

"Full time?"

"Yes. You want this thing solved quickly, don't you? Buddy, pal."

Wilson tensed his body then settled back into his chair. "You know what, Barnett? I'm going to give you everything you want. You want Quill off, I'll arrange it somehow. Know why?" He leaned forward. "I don't want to hear you bitch that I didn't support you in this investigation after you fall flat on your face." He picked up an imaginary phone. "I want to be able to go to the chief and say, 'Of course I gave him the resources he asked for. Yes, sir. I even took our most senior man from Mobile Crime and put him at Barnett's disposal twenty-four hours a day. I know it's unheard of, but Barnett assured us that's what he needed to solve this case. Yes, sir. I'll put someone else on it. And, sir, Barnett will be happy to look for your daughter's Toyota. He'll be assigned to Auto this afternoon.'" Wilson smiled widely.

Barnett got up. "Captain, you're the best pal a cop could have. I take back all the bad things I ever said about you."

"Get out of here."

Nobody moved.

"Out, out."

When they were clear of the office Barnett laughed loudly.

"Why do you torture that man, Mike?"

"It's a hobby. I can't seem to get interested in collecting stamps or porcelain figurines."

Cag pushed the elevator button. "If I ever make Captain, will you drive me crazy, too?"

"Probably not, Cag. By that time, I'll be well into my stamp collection."

Chapter 47

"What's this all over the equipment?" Quill said. With a look of disgust he flicked hair off the camcorders. "Yech."

"Don't complain," Barnett said. He pulled a list from his pocket, checking the models off as he helped Quill take them out of the box onto the workbench. "I had to use the K-9 station wagon."

"I can't believe you got me off my regular gig. What's it gonna cost me?"

"You? Nothing. Me and Cag, our livelihoods."

"Don't worry dear friend," Quill said with his hand on his heart. "I won't let you down."

"Cut the shit. When do you want some more?"

"As fast as you can bring them. It only takes about a half-hour to check each unit, but there's about three hundred models out there. With any luck we won't have to check too many before we get a match. I'm concentrating on the popular ones first." He reached into a cooler under the table and pulled out a beer. "So I don't have to go upstairs. Want one?"

Barnett laughed. "No. I'm heading back downtown. If there are any models that you need that we don't have, let me know and I'll rent it. Wilson gave me a few bucks.''

"He's not taking any chances. He's gonna nail your ass if it doesn't work, isn't he?''

"That's the plan.''

Barnett made two more round trips to the property room then stopped in at Auto. He saw Kirk. "What's the story?''

"We're clearing the decks now. Your job gets priority,'' said Kirk, "but it's going to take time. Simple but time-consuming. First we'll check for green Jags: the District and the burbs. When we get the owners' names, we'll cross-check them with the driver's license list of those with red hair. That takes extra time 'cause a lot of people have District licenses but register their cars outside to save on insurance.''

Simpson, sitting at the next desk, added, "It's also routine to disregard female hair information on licenses. Too many dye jobs.''

Kirk continued. "There's another problem I know we'll run into. Cars like Jags, Rolls, and Mercedes are usually leased or company owned. We'll have to track down the actual drivers by hand.''

"Word is you got Quill full time. That true?'' asked Simpson.

"True. When will I see something?''

"Five days if we rush,'' Simpson said. "How'd you do that?''

Barnett crossed his fingers. "Captain Wilson and I are like that. There's nothing he wouldn't do for me.''

"Don't forget us, Barnett. We're on your side all the way,'' Kirk said.

Simpson looked up. "All the way.''

Barnett headed back to his office. He didn't know what else to do but wait. He didn't like the feeling of inaction so he decided to work on his mail.

His cubbyhole was stuffed, and it took some twisting and turning to pull out the load. There were several phone messages jammed between the letters and magazines. He made piles of material to keep and throw out.

His eyes stopped on one phone message from a woman with an odd name. He was about to call her back when he realized it wasn't for him.

He got up to put it in Caggiano's box when he came out of his office. "Got this by mistake."

Caggiano took the message without looking at it. "And this is for you. It's the letter the mayor got."

Barnett opened the envelope and read the short message aloud. "Ready for the big finish? I am." The wire was in a small Ziploc bag. He looked at Caggiano. "I don't think we need to check the wire do you?"

Caggiano didn't answer. He was mesmerized by the phone message slip.

"Cag? The wire. Should we check it or not?"

"What? Uh, no. You're right. Not necessary."

"Who's the woman? Is that your mysterious lady friend?"

"She's never called here before," he whispered.

"What?" said Barnett. "Didn't hear you."

"Never mind." Caggiano walked quickly into his office and closed the door. He let the number ring twenty or so times, then he dialed it again, slowly, carefully. He reread the message while it rang. "Call back as soon as possible." It was dated yesterday.

A woman answered.

"Damian?"

"No, Marjorie." She slurred the words.

"Is Damian there?"

"Could be. There's a lot of people around here. It's a goddamn phone booth, buster." She slammed the receiver down.

Chapter 48

Marybeth Wolfe pulled her green Jaguar into the parking lot at Union Station, strolled through the shops, and settled into America for a drink. She wore a leather miniskirt, a white cashmere sweater, and black high heels. The kitchen staff peered out the door one by one to watch her sip champagne until the manager shooed them back amongst the pots and pans.

She looked at her watch every few minutes, glanced around furtively, then finally motioned for the check. At exactly 4:20 she left a big tip and walked outside towards the Capitol.

The streets were relatively empty for a Friday afternoon, Congressional workers getting in their last minute phone calls and catching up on paperwork before heading out for the weekend.

The guard at the Dirkson building stared as she stepped through the metal detector and watched as she strode through the hall with authority. She knew exactly where she was going.

About a block away, a knot of students were playing Monkey In The Middle with Tommy Bizjak's Orioles cap. They made fun of the mildly retarded boy, whose brown eyes were magnified by thick glasses. As the boys and girls tossed his cap around, laughing and jumping, he tried to grab it back, but his spastic movements only made them laugh even more and hold the hat that much longer, teasing and tormenting him to where he sat down on the pavement and cried.

Suddenly, the joking stopped as a large man stepped out of the school building and confronted the tiny students. The circle parted as the man pointed to the boy holding the cap and screamed for him to give it to Tommy. The boy responded immediately and walked sheepishly towards the hysterical Tommy.

"You and you," the man said to two girls on the periphery. "Help him up."

"But we didn't do anything," one of them said.

"Do as I say! And do it now!"

The man waited patiently as they tried to lift little Tommy by his arms, but the boy wouldn't let them touch him. "I can do it myself. Leave me alone." He put his cap on his head crookedly, found his books, and stomped away trying to muster what little dignity he had left.

The angry man looked around and pointed. "I want you, you, and you to the principal's office."

"But we—" one of the girls said.

"Now!"

The girls looked at each other, terrified. "I think he's the gym teacher for the older boys," one said. "I heard he's really mean."

"No talking." The man folded his arms watching the three cowering, walking toward the building. "You. Don't I know you?"

"I don't think so."

"Yes, I do. You're Carol and Mike Barnett's daughter, aren't you?"

Penny stood petrified.

"Your father's a police officer, isn't he? I think I'll take you directly to your mother on my way home. She works for Senator Olson, doesn't she?"

"Yes."

"The rest of you inside and be thankful your mothers don't work nearby. Go!"

"Let's go, young lady. We'll see what your mother has to say about this."

Al Olson's office was decorated with posters of his home state of Wyoming which made a low-rent contrast against the nicely paneled walls. The office was divided into cubicles, each having a word processor and several in-out baskets. Papers and newspaper clippings were thumbtacked to the outside of each one.

"Harlan's in the building today," Marybeth said to Carol Barnett. "We've got tickets for the Kennedy Center tonight. Is it okay if I wait here for him?"

"Sure," said Carol. "It's nice to see you again. How is Harlan?"

Marybeth didn't have time to respond. Carol signaled with her finger to hold the thought as she answered the phone. Her face registered terror. "What? Where? How long ago? I'll be right there."

"What happened?" asked Marybeth.

"The school. My daughter, Penny, she . . . I have to get there immediately."

"Let me take you in a cab. Come on."

As the two hustled outside, Marybeth pointed to a car just pulling into a space. "Look, it's Harlan. Great timing."

Carol thought it was a little odd that she and Marybeth both squeezed into the back seat, but she didn't dwell on it for more than an instant before she blacked out.

The last thing she remembered was Marybeth's hand smoothing the front of her blouse.

The messenger wore bicycle shorts, racing shoes, and carried a knapsack with a tire pump sticking out of the top. He double-checked the address on the package before he spoke. "Detective Barnett, Homicide. Right?"

The secretary put her pencil down on the find-a-word magazine and took the envelope. She signed the receipt book and buzzed Barnett on the intercom.

He was glad for the diversion as he bounded to the front office. It had been four days since he set Quill and the two men from Auto loose and he hadn't heard a word. "Whatcha got for me, Liz? Something good, I hope."

He thought it might be from Quill and eagerly clawed at the flap. He looked at Liz, who was waiting for him to open it. "Maybe it's from Carol. A love letter."

Liz lost her interest. "Nobody ever sends me nothing."

Barnett reached inside but couldn't feel anything. "Hmm." Liz was interested again. He dug deeper.

His smile disappeared as he slowly pulled out the prize.

"What the hell is that?" said Liz.

Barnett stood paralyzed, Penny's panda bookmark in his hand, a thin, shiny wire wrapped around its neck.

Chapter 49

Caggiano milled around the phone booth from which she had called him. Graffiti covered the booth's glass; the inside reeked of urine. He couldn't remember if he had changed his clothes since he started his search for Damian. He felt his face and was sure he hadn't shaved for at least two days.

He walked to a trick pad she sometimes used and was met by a doorman who some tenants paid regularly to send word upstairs whenever a suit came snooping around. Caggiano smiled, said hello, and stretched the man's right nostril with the barrel of a nine millimeter. Standing on his tiptoes, the man squealed that he hadn't seen Damian for at least five days. No one had come calling for her in that period either.

Caggiano surprised himself that he could work up his anger so quickly yet stay calmly detached from the situation. He hadn't done something like that in years, not since he had worked the streets. He wasn't bothered by his instant brutality even though a flash of his badge would've accomplished the same thing.

The only feeling that lingered as he walked

away was annoyance that the doorman didn't know more.

He spent the following days and nights walking the streets although his instinct told him it was useless. Nobody had seen her, not even her buddies who were worried about her too. But not worried enough to call the police.

She might be dying, stuffed under a bed by a john who went ape shit. Was it the man in the cowboy hat? He strained his memory. What kind of car was it?

Maybe she was already dead, lying peacefully in a refrigerator drawer waiting for someone to claim her body.

Later that afternoon, the morgue attendant said the description Caggiano gave him over the phone fit at least two women. Both had been brought in within the past several days, murdered and unclaimed. He checked his clipboard then motioned for Caggiano to follow.

Caggiano sighed with relief as the attendant picked up the white sheet over the second corpse. "No. That's not her either," he said softly.

"Have you checked the hospitals?" the attendant said.

"I would if I knew her real name."

"Okay," the attendant said, drawing out the second syllable.

Caggiano would need help if he was going to check all the hospitals. Who could he ask who wouldn't want to know why he didn't know the woman's name? Who could he trust not to judge him?

He would have to do it himself.

Caggiano checked DC General first, talking to the

emergency room people, reading the long list of admissions over the past several days. He marked those that might be Damian and began checking their rooms, starting with Intensive Care.

He walked from bed to bed, amid the tangle of wires, tubes and hanging bags, studying the black-and-blue faces. Some of them looked up in anticipation of a loved one, then wearily turned away when there was no recognition.

Then he saw her.

Bandages covered her head. Her arms and legs were in casts. Her swollen eyes were slits.

"Damian," he whispered.

Her head turned towards him. Tears coursed down her cheeks.

"Oh, John. I . . . hurt," she whispered.

Caggiano touched her fingertips. "What happened? Who did this to you?"

Her face squeezed shut in pain.

"Do you know who did this?"

"Regular trick . . . went crazy . . . I—"

"Who, Damian, who?"

Damian passed out before she could say anything.

"That woman over there," he asked the nurse.

"Beaten badly. Arms and legs broken. Internal damage." She held his arm. "We've been waiting for someone to come. Are you family?"

"A friend."

"We're doing everything we can, but she's in bad shape. There might be brain damage. We don't know yet. The next few days will tell. Can we have your name in case—you know."

Mechanically, he handed her his card.

"All right, Lieutenant," she said, reading. "We'll call you if there's any change."

Caggiano stood at her bedside and held her fingers. "I don't know what to say, Damian, except . . . I love you. When you get better I promise to make an honest woman of you. I love you, Damian. I love you."

Caggiano thought he felt her squeeze his fingers.

Chapter 50

Barnett still held the bookmark in his hand when he rushed towards Caggiano's office.

"Don't bother," the officer said. "He's been out for days."

"Where?" Barnett said, almost out of breath.

The officer shrugged.

Barnett tried to slow his mind. He'd been going full bore, running around the office since talking to Penny's school then learning about Carol's hasty exit from work. Was Caggiano missing too?

A few minutes later he burst into Wilson's office. "They have my daughter, my wife, maybe Cag," he said.

Wilson looked stunned. "I know about Cag. He wanted a couple of days off and looked like he needed it. What's this about Carol and your daughter?"

Barnett explained.

Wilson dialed the phone and looked at Barnett solidly. "Barnett, listen, we've had our disagreements, but we take care of our own. You can have anything and anyone you want. You know that."

Wilson handed Barnett the phone. "It's Caggiano," he said.

"Cag. They've got Penny and Carol."

"What? Who?"

"Our killers."

"Calm down. Tell me the whole story."

Wilson called Communications from his other phone. He ordered the dispatcher to have every detective not attending a crime scene to report to Headquarters.

Wilson looked at Barnett. "I'll brief them when they call in. Give me descriptions. We'll find them, Barnett. Don't worry. We'll find them."

Barnett hit his fist into his palm. He was frozen in his seat wanting to go . . . but where?

The first calls from detectives came within minutes and Wilson immediately dispatched a team to the school and another to Carol's office. He did it so quickly that Barnett hardly noticed. "That's taken care of," said Wilson. "Have you heard from Quill or Auto?"

"I'm going there now," Barnett said, rushing out the door.

"Barnett!" Liz the secretary screamed. "There's a fax for you."

Paper was strewn on the floor, and more was being pumped out. He read the first page: "Barnett: Knew you wanted this stuff fast. I'm in New Jersey at the R. W. Jones Fulfillment Company. They handle warranty lists for Panasonic. I'm sure it's the PV510 model. The list is sorted by zip code. Work from the top down. Be back tonight." It was signed Quill.

When the fax stopped, Barnett ripped it off and headed for Auto.

Chapter 51

The room was bright. The tiled floor was white, clean, cold. The bookshelves that lined three walls were bare. As she picked herself off the floor, the side of her face felt numb. She touched her cheek, and her fingers seemed to sink in several inches before she sensed them.

She sat cross-legged, her head spinning. Her balance still off, she couldn't find anything in the room to focus on, to help her adjust. She didn't remember arriving at this . . . what was it . . . a vacant house?

She tried to stand and walk but took two steps and collapsed in a heap.

Her thoughts returned in fragments. Penny's school called . . . Marybeth Wolfe . . . her husband's car.

She shook her head and the stark room became clearer. The lines and angles became sharper.

Penny! What happened to Penny?

Shaking it off again, Carol stumbled to her feet and lurched for the one blank wall. She concentrated on each step. She patted the wall with her palms. Nothing. Her patting turned to frantic slapping. Where was the door?

She spun around and stared at the bookcases. Her vision was still blurred. Carol squinted, trying to focus.

Gripping the shelves like a mountain climber, she staggered from stack to stack, looking for a crack, a seam, anything that would indicate a door.

Taking a rest, clutching a shelf, she felt a warm flow of air on her face. Peering in between the shelves, her eyes registered a dark vertical line.

She pulled on the stacks desperately, but nothing happened. She rocked it back and forth with all her strength but could manage nothing.

Exhausted, Carol sat on the floor, her back against the shelf. She was breathing hard.

Suddenly, the shelf swung open and she was being pushed across the tiles. She tried to get up but couldn't get a purchase on the floor. Then she tried to stop herself from moving by digging in her heels, but each time a tile edge caught, the force behind the bookcase pushed harder.

Then, all movement ceased. She waited, crossing her arms in front of her body, tensing her muscles.

Nobody entered.

She got up and peered around the edge of the bookcase.

All she could see was darkness.

All she could hear were echoing footsteps getting smaller in the distance.

Chapter 52

"I'm out of time," Barnett said solemnly.

Kirk put down his sandwich and looked at Barnett. "We're spitting out the last half of the Maryland burbs right now. Simpson's already out tracking down the lease jobs we turned up. My guess is about twenty possibles." He wiped his mouth.

"They've got my wife and daughter," Barnett said softly.

Kirk winced, stood up to face Barnett. "We're moving as fast as we can. I promise you." The two stared at each other awkwardly. Finally Kirk pointed to the papers in Barnett's hand. "What's that?"

"Possibles based on some work Quill was doing. I want to cross them with your list."

Kirk reached out and took the continuous sheet of paper and scrolled it up in his hands. "I'll take care of it." He patted Barnett on the shoulder. "Mike, this is all we can do right now."

"I know. I know."

The phone rang and Kirk grabbed it. "It's Captain Wilson."

"Barnett here."

"According to Penny's classmates, she was last

seen walking away with a red-haired man. Nobody saw a car. The kids were too scared to give a description."

Barnett's body tensed. "And Carol's office?"

"You know it all already." Wilson paused. "A red-haired woman."

Barnett felt sweat dripping down his face. Confirmation. Absolute.

"What do you want to do now?" Wilson asked.

"I don't know what else to do except wait." He put the phone down slowly. Kirk was already typing at a keyboard several desks away. The fax paper roll was draped over the desk and his head bobbed up and down.

Barnett stood in the middle of the room. He felt alone and helpless, spent. Where were they? Were they all right? Was he hurting them? Barnett put his hand over his eyes and rubbed. It ended with his fingers over the bridge of his nose.

My fault. My fault. Frank, Carol, Penny . . .

"Barnett," someone shouted from the hall. It was Caggiano.

The two walked towards each other and looked like they were going to hug. Instead, Caggiano grabbed Barnett's hand between his two hands and squeezed. "It'll be okay, Mike."

"When I find this bastard I'm going to—"

"It's not going to work that way," Caggiano said. "You know that. You might not even be the one to get to him first. Maybe somebody else will."

"I can't help thinking that—"

Kirk screamed across the room. 'Simpson just called. He's done with the leases. One hour. That's all we need."

Barnett didn't say anything.

"Wilson's assembling a team to handle the warrants."

"Warrants?!" Barnett said. Caggiano jumped.

"Calm down. It'll be fast. We won't waste any time."

Barnett stood motionless.

"By the book, Mike. By the book. Want to lose this?"

Barnett didn't say anything. He stomped into the bathroom and looked in the mirror. His eyes were red. His body was shaking. He put his right hand under his arm and felt that his gun was there.

Caggiano went in after him, but Barnett was already gone.

Chapter 53

Feeling her way along the darkened corridor, Carol headed towards the sound of footsteps which abruptly stopped. Squinting, she saw a pinhole of light ahead and slowly made for it.

Suddenly, an odor of musty, wet blankets engulfed her, making her nauseous. She rested until the wave subsided; then she continued.

The light was coming through a keyhole. She gripped the knob and listened. On the other side, a child was sobbing.

Carol twisted the knob viciously and ripped the door open in one continuous movement.

"Penny!" The little girl was handcuffed to a chair, her mouth covered with wide tape. Her hair was mussed, dirty.

Penny's eyes widened and looked beyond her mother in fear. Carol held her tiny face in her hands, and the girl's mouth tried to scream as the tape was pulled from her lips, but no sound came out.

"Oh, baby. Are you all right?"

Penny twitched and continued to stare past Carol.

"Penny, Penny. Speak to me. Are you all right?"

"She's fine," the voice behind her said. "She's just a little scared."

Carol jumped and turned.

"But I guess you would be too, under the circumstances."

"Harlan Wolfe!" Trembling, Carol had trouble getting the words out. "What . . . ?"

"It's coming to a close, dear Carol."

Carol stood between Wolfe and Penny, hiding the little girl from the man's view.

"Nothing's worked so far. It takes a lot for me, I guess. It's just my lot in life. Nothing I can do about it. Blame it on my genes, my upbringing, who knows?"

"What . . . what are you talking about?" she managed.

"Come on, Carol," he said impatiently. "You know. The women. Henkel. They were all part of my life." He hesitated. "For a short while at least."

Carol kept sidestepping, keeping herself between him and Penny as Wolfe strolled around the room. He stopped and examined a jade vase. It was the first time Carol actually noticed anything in the room except Penny and Wolfe. She was in a tastefully decorated study with bookcases stocked with gold-leaf bound books. Oil paintings illuminated by their own lamps hung on the walls. The furniture—a sofa, a loveseat—was leather. An antique rolltop desk fit snugly in the corner.

"You know, Carol," he began calmly, "when you read the literature, I'm a rather textbook type. That's always distressed me—being so, you know, predictable, shall we say? On the other hand, I've always taken great pride in the way I've handled myself. I like to think of myself as having a gracious lifestyle. Look around. Don't you agree?"

"What do you want?"

Wolfe's voice filled with anger. "Business, business, business. Always back to business. No time for leisure. Push, push, push—"

"I didn't mean to—"

"Didn't mean to what? To set me off, to get me crazy? You know, Carol, it's nothing personal. You must believe me. It's just that your husband is the best around, and if I don't tackle the best then why bother? Plus, he understands, what with his brother and all. You can see that, can't you?"

Carol kept her eyes glued to Wolfe. Her hands behind her were gripping Penny's arms which were still handcuffed to the chair.

"Why not let her go? She hasn't done anything. She's just a child."

"Just a child! Do you know what I did when I was just a child? Do you have any idea?" He stomped around the room erratically, then stopped at the bookcase where he retrieved a black binder. "Sit on the couch."

Carol didn't move.

"Sit. I won't hurt her or you." He thrust the book at her. "Here, read this."

Carol kept still.

He tossed it on the couch and headed for the door. "I'll be back."

Once the door closed, Carol got down to Penny's level. "Darling, say something. Speak to me."

Penny didn't respond. She was in shock. All she could do was whimper. Carol tried to release the handcuffs but couldn't. She tugged and tugged.

With reserve strength she ran to the door and pulled. It was locked from the outside.

Carol looked back at Penny then over to the couch where the book landed. Its cover was open, and she could see a plastic sleeve with a newspaper clipping neatly cut and centered in it.

She went to the couch and placed it on her lap. She read the first clip. It was nearly twenty-two years old. "He was just a teenager," she whispered to herself.

The book was thick, and as she turned the pages she became more horrified with each clip. She looked up at Penny, who was shivering. She looked back at the book.

Her hands began to shake so much she could barely read the succession of news accounts and psychiatric reports that followed.

When she finally reached the last page, she sat motionless, her body sinking farther into the couch as her body went limp.

She looked again at Penny and went to her. Kneeling, she put her head in the girl's lap.

Harlan Wolfe watched the scene from behind the gilded two-way mirror on the opposite side of the room and grinned.

Chapter 54

"She asked for you, Lieutenant," the nurse said. "I called you immediately."

"How much time does she have left?"

"I'm sorry." She touched his chest and looked into his eyes. "We don't know. Go see her."

Caggiano stood beside the bed as the nurse pulled the privacy curtain around them.

Damian turned her head. She didn't recognize him immediately. He waited quietly until she did. "John . . . I'm glad . . . you're here." Her mouth strained to form a smile. Her eyelids were half-closed.

"Is there anyone you want me to call?"

She managed a tiny laugh. "There's . . . no one." She coughed and took a hard breath. He caressed her forehead, pushing her hair off her face.

"Damian. Who did this? What happened?"

"I . . ." She coughed again. "Told you. Regular . . . went . . . too far . . ."

"Who Damian, who?"

"Closer . . ."

Caggiano put his ear to her mouth, and he felt puffs of air as she whispered to him. Moments later, without warning, she gasped, coughed.

The ECG machine emitted a buzz.

Within seconds, two nurses and a doctor tore open the curtain and pushed Caggiano aside. "Please wait outside," one of them ordered as they hovered over her body.

Caggiano heard them snap commands at each other as he walked away.

In the hall, he sat on a red plastic chair and thought about what it was like to die without family around.

The doctor approached him twenty minutes later. "I'm sorry. We did all we could. Are you a relative?"

"No . . . yes. I am."

The doctor shot him a suspicious look and cleared his throat. "The nurse's station has forms for . . . for a family member to fill out." He pointed to a semicircular desk in the middle of the hall. "You'll need to show them identification. Will that be a problem?"

"No problem."

"I'm very sorry. The beating she received was too severe. She died of internal bleeding. I'm sorry." With that, he walked away.

Caggiano rested his arms on the counter, and when the nurse acknowledged his presence he said, "I want to make some arrangements."

Chapter 55

Barnett and Caggiano met in the hall. They had both responded to calls from Wilson to return to the office.

"You smell, Mike."

"You're not so sweet yourself, Cag."

"How was the range?"

Barnett sniffed his hands. The odor of cordite lingered. "I had to do something. I couldn't just sit around."

"Don't do anything crazy, Mike. We all want this guy bad, but don't do something you'll regret."

Barnett huffed. "You're too educated to rely on clichés, Cag." They entered the elevator.

"I mean it, Mike," said Caggiano as he pressed the button.

"It's my wife and daughter we're talking about."

"I know that. We all know that. But if you blow someone away and—"

The door opened.

"Let's go," Barnett said. They stopped short of the door to the Line-up room, which was used for briefings. Barnett held the doorknob but didn't turn it. He looked at Caggiano. "You been to the morgue?"

"Why do you say that?"

"I smell something medicinal."

"It's not from me," Caggiano said. "Get inside."

The room lacked the usual electricity preceding a bust. Kirk, Simpson, and Wilson were quietly chatting in the front of the room. On the podium lay folded legal documents.

"No need to sit down," Wilson said as the two men from Auto gravitated to Caggiano and Barnett. "Each team will have one detective and four patrol officers," Wilson said. "We haven't scoped out the houses, so once you're there, call for additional men if you think you need it."

Wilson shuffled the papers in his hands like he was working a card trick. "There's only four locations in the District that fit the parameters. When and if you're done with your scene, you'll be assigned to back up the one nearest you. I'll be on SOD channel. The ERT team will be available."

Wilson handed the papers to Caggiano. He carefully checked the names on all the warrants, buried one in his pocket, and distributed the rest. "Remember, we have four people with the right car and the right video camera, but they all can't be murderers. In fact, none of them may be our subject." He looked at Barnett and held the glance. "Do I make myself clear?"

Barnett barely heard the last words. He was already halfway out the door.

Chapter 56

"It won't be long now," said Harlan Wolfe. "As soon as Marybeth returns, we'll be ready."

Carol was nude, her arms and legs bound spread-eagle on a mattress. Her right side felt hot from a kleig lamp mounted on a tripod. Sweat dripped down her inner thighs.

"Smile," he said from behind the camera. He turned knobs. "Good."

He shut off the lights and a dark chill immediately penetrated Carol's skin, causing her to tremble.

The only illumination came from a tree lamp standing in the corner. It cast stickmenlike shadows of the equipment on the walls.

"Why?" she cried. "Why are you . . . ?" She strained at her bonds.

Wolfe settled into an overstuffed chair near the prostrate woman. "You read my scrapbook. You saw the newspaper clips and the medical reports." He crossed his legs. "You tell me."

Carol tried to put her subservient state out of her mind as she began talking. "It was terrible what your father did to you—"

"To us. What he did to *us.*"

"Right. You and your sister. It was awful."

"You don't know how it was." Wolfe stood up and marched around the room. "Every day. Every day. Either her or me. One of us. We never spoke about it when it first began." Wolfe stopped in front of Carol. He looked down and pointed his finger. "I was the man. I should have saved her."

"But you couldn't have. You were a child. He was an adult. You couldn't do anything."

"And Mother. Why didn't she stop it? Why didn't she help us? Tell me that!"

"Don't you think she would have if she could? She was scared of him, too. Don't you see that?"

"Oh, sure. You're like the rest of them. The doctors, the therapists. Detached, clinical. You weren't there. None of you were there! We—" He poked at his chest. "We were there. We knew what it felt like. You, you and your PhDs and your medical licenses. Yeah, you know it all. Don't you?" He charged around Carol. She twisted her neck in all directions to keep up with his movements.

"He tried to kill us. Did you know that? He tried, oh yeah, he tried, but he didn't succeed. Do you know why? Do you know why? Because we were too smart for him. We saw through the plan. Ha. He thought it would work, but we were too smart for him."

Carol saw him disappear into the other room. He came back a minute later holding a box. "It was the cereal. He tried to use the cereal, but it didn't work. It didn't work. Ha!" He ripped open the box and swung it around the room. Cereal pieces sprayed. When no more came out, he threw the box against the wall. It bounced and landed on Carol's stomach. She squirmed, tried to shake it off, but it stuck.

Wolfe loomed over her. "We took care of him,

286

didn't we?'' He lowered his body over hers. She felt his breath. "Didn't we?''

"Yes, yes. You did. But now its over. It's all over.''

"Over? Ha. It's not over. Not until we get it right. Not until it's all settled. Smooth in my mind. Not until we get it the way it should be. It's not resolved yet. No. I haven't found my peace. Not yet. That's what you're here for. You're going to help us make it right for once and all. Not like the others. You'll say it's okay.''

His last comment confused Carol. She pulled at her restraints. His eyes were shining at her.

Suddenly, as if somebody pulled a switch, he stood up. His legs were still straddling her. His body became relaxed, and he looked down at Carol without a hint of recognition. He carefully lifted his right foot taking pains not to touch her.

"You'll excuse me please. I have some house chores to attend to.''

With that, he walked away. The door closed, leaving Carol surrounded by the stickmen on the walls.

Chapter 57

Kirk showed his nervousness by wringing his hands over the steering wheel. The detective was half hoping he would draw a blank on the suspects even though a well-done job might be his ticket out of Auto.

Two cruisers followed close behind and the caravan stopped about a block from the house. Kirk checked the address three times before he assured himself that he was at the right location. He hadn't worked a "no-knock" warrant since he was in Vice, and it made him nervous.

There was no way to reach the back of the row house without attracting attention. Kirk decided to go in the front.

As he peered through the front window, he saw a red-headed man preparing food in the kitchen. If he was holding two women in the house, would he be that calm?

Kirk's instinct told him not to assume anything. He had one of the officers change places with him, keeping his eye on the man, while he worked on the door. He was sure he could crowbar the door in one swift move before the man knew what was happening. If he bolted and ran, they would forget the smooth stuff, bash in the door, and be all over him in less than twenty seconds.

Kirk glanced at the officer under the window. He mouthed, "Ready?" The officer nodded.

Kirk took a deep breath, inserted the bar between the door and jamb, and yanked.

Caggiano studied the red-brick house for ten minutes before deciding how to approach it. His plan was to place two men in the rear alley, one covering the basement exit on the side and the other going with him through the front door. He decided not to cover the garage. Instead, he was going to park his car close enough so if the door was raised, the outside handle would catch on the bottom of the bumper and stop.

The house had recently been rehabbed. In fact, all the houses on the block had been refurbished within the past several years by young upper-class white couples who had turned the neighborhood from a forgotten slum into a desirable area. What distressed Caggiano about these structures was their size. Most were three stories, and that left too much time for someone to barricade himself and his hostages in a well-protected room upstairs.

Another thing troubled him. Burglar bars covered every window and door.

The more he looked at the house, the more it spooked him. After going over a possible scenario in his mind, Caggiano requested extra men. The only way to handle it was to break down all the doors with battering rams and have officers enter the second and third-floor windows by way of the fire escape.

He wasn't embarrassed to be so careful. From his car, Caggiano watched the house and thought about what was going on inside.

Within five minutes, three additional cruisers arrived, and Caggiano immediately deployed the officers.

They stood at their posts ready for Caggiano's signal. He silently prayed as he pressed the button on his walkie-talkie.

"Go."

Simpson considered himself lucky. The address turned out to be a large Victorian in upper Northwest. The house sat on a fenced lot that allowed open views. The two-car garage was recessed in from the street.

The wooden doors, front and rear, would give way easily to a ram.

The officers stood in the front and rear ready for his signal. He was certain they hadn't been seen.

Simpson had the feeling that no one was home. He tried to look through the garage windows, but they were covered with curtains. The place was quiet.

Just as he was about to give the signal to enter, something caught Simpson's eye. On the side of the house, the hurricane door leading to the basement rose.

Simpson ran to it, trying not to make any noise. He pointed his shotgun at the door and held his breath. The door lowered. He tensed as it raised again.

Finally, with a single movement, the door swung open and a red-headed man emerged, oblivious to the steel barrel only inches from his head.

Simpson's finger, wrapped around the trigger, strained and twitched.

Barnett stopped his car and ducked under the dash

as soon as he saw the woman turn into the garage. He counted to ten and lifted his head just enough to see the automatic door close in front of a green Jaguar and a small white compact berthed next to it.

He didn't get a look at the woman.

In the middle of the street, a C&P Telephone truck had set up a yellow tent above a manhole. A rubber pipe resembling a monstrous caterpillar was transporting air from a noisy motor to the workers underneath the street.

Barnett looked around and at the house before scurrying inside the tent.

"Hey, you can't go in there," shouted a man wearing yellow overalls, work boots, and a white hard hat. "Hey, you."

"Get in," said Barnett as he pulled the man towards him.

Inside the tent, Barnett produced his badge. "I need your help. I have to get inside that house over there." He pointed. "How long you been set up out here?"

The man didn't answer.

"How long?"

"Three days."

"Perfect. Let me borrow your clothes."

"C'mon. I can't do that."

"Look, buddy. This is a police matter. I need your clothes."

"I don't know—"

Barnett pulled open his coat exposing his shoulder holster. "This isn't some bullshit fun and games."

The man turned pale. "Okay. You got it." He began peeling off his gear.

After he placed the hard hat on his head, Barnett turned around to the man who was now wearing his jacket. "Sit tight," he said. "Keep your head down."

When the officers saw Barnett in his new outfit heading for the house, they started to follow. He shot them a furtive glance and motioned with his hands for them to stay where they were. The men looked at each other confused and reluctantly retreated to their cars.

Barnett squared his shoulders and ran up the front steps. He got to the top, surveyed the street, felt under his arm.

He rang the bell.

Inside, a woman's voice said she would be right there.

The door opened.

Chapter 58

The radio calls came in quick succession. Simpson was the first.

The owner of the Victorian house was too shocked to rant about police brutality in the form of a shotgun being pointed at him. In addition, Simpson was able to placate the man by describing how he was only one of four people in the District who fit a very special set of parameters that included the cereal killer.

For reasons that Simpson couldn't fathom, the attention made the red-headed man feel important.

Passport stamps convinced Simpson that the suspect was out of the country during the first two murders. And the man's teenaged daughter swore that her father was indeed traveling overseas.

Still, Simpson searched the house thoroughly, confiscated his camcorder for Quill and kept two officers outside the house until ordered to do otherwise.

On the other side of the city, Kirk stood over the felled front door as a red-haired man lunged at him with a large kitchen knife. The detective was able to sidestep and watch him fall on his face. Looking up with a bloodied mouth, the man dropped the knife when he spotted the uniformed officers.

Cuffed and forced to his feet, the man looked at the search warrant.

"Me, a murderer?" he said. His lip was growing in size as Kirk and he talked, and the officers searched the house. "I've never even had a parking ticket."

A search of his desk showed the man to be a consultant working out of his house. An appointment book indicated that he had recently purchased a green Jaguar. Too recently.

"Just got it last week," he said. "It's new."

Kirk looked at the man's expanding lip. "Shit."

The ambulance arrived and the paramedics tore through the doorway carrying their equipment. "What's all this?" said a large black paramedic in a white outfit examining the two splintered halves of the door. "Drug bust? In this neighborhood?"

Kirk uncuffed the man, handed him to the attendants. "Take good care of him."

The man, shocked and aching, lowered his eyes to his chest as Kirk dropped a business card in his breast pocket. From the phone, Kirk called Wilson and explained the situation. "I'll keep a man here until the door is repaired."

Kirk took the camcorder, placed it in the trunk of his car, and headed for Caggiano's location. He was only a few minutes behind Simpson.

As he drove away, he thought about a Vice detective named Walters who did a no-knock on a suspected crack house that turned out to belong to a councilwoman's arthritic mother. As far as he knew, Walters was still permanently assigned to high school drug prevention programs.

Barnett reported next. The woman who answered the door was surprisingly cordial when Barnett told

296

her why he was there.

"Really?" she said, eyeing his telephone company uniform and his badge and trying to reconcile the two. "And what makes you think my husband and I are murderers?"

She was a little too collected for Barnett, who made the decision not to call for backup from the officers outside. He inquired if anyone else was in the house.

"Yes. I believe my husband is downstairs. Would you like me to call him?"

Barnett grabbed the woman's left arm, twisted it behind her and stuck his revolver in her back. "We'll go there together."

Pushing the now indignant woman in front of him, they walked down the stairs. At the bottom, he said: "Call him."

The woman was frightened. "Honey."

No response.

"Sometimes he gets absorbed in his work."

"Again," he commanded.

"Honey!"

This time a man answered. "Be right there. I've got some beautiful things for you here."

Barnett stood behind the woman, tightening his grip.

In a dark corner of the basement, a curtain rustled and a man in a wheelchair rolled through. "What the—"

Barnett uncocked his revolver.

Chapter 59

"What the—"

Wolfe, standing alone in his bedroom, was taken by surprise. Caggiano screamed: "Don't move a muscle."

Wolfe froze and held his hands up.

"Where are they?"

"Where're who?"

"Barnett's wife, the girl. Where?"

"I don't know what you're talking about."

Just then a voice on the walkie-talkie: "We got them both Lieutenant. They're okay. Shaken up bad but okay."

Caggiano smiled. "You're lucky I got to you before Barnett did."

"I feel real lucky," Wolfe said snidely.

Caggiano looked around. The dresser and headboard were exquisitely carved mahogany. A mirror covered one wall. Formal clothes were laid out on the bed.

"Going out?"

"We were just planning an evening at home."

"Where is she?"

Wolfe didn't answer and turned his head.

"Let's go."

Caggiano was deadpan as he led Harlan Wolfe out the front door in handcuffs. Wolfe was smirking at the crowd who had gathered on the sidewalk to gawk.

He threw Wolfe to an officer. "Put him in, Starr. I'll be right back."

The inside of the house was quiet with only a few men standing around. "Nobody touches anything until Mobile Crime arrives," Caggiano said as he entered. Walking over to Carol and Penny, he put on a big smile. "We got him. Everything's okay now."

Carol, wrapped in a blanket, held Penny as the girl cried uncontrollably. "I knew him, John," Carol said slowly. She shuddered as she spoke. "He said he was going to use me for—I don't know. He had a camera and everything set up. If Marybeth had come back, I'd be—"

Caggiano put his hand on her shoulder. "I know, Carol. Take it easy. I heard on the radio that Mike is on his way." He looked at Penny who was buried in her mother's arm. "Dad will be here soon, Penny. He'll take you home." His soft tone did little to calm the little girl who was now crying in fits and starts.

Carol rocked her back and forth.

"I'm taking him in before Mike sees him."

In the car, Caggiano looked back through the cage at a grinning Wolfe then to Starr. "Let's go."

They drove several blocks. Caggiano mindlessly looked out the window until his eye caught Starr's foot slam on the brake pedal. Wolfe groaned as he was thrown forward.

Before them was a fresh two-car accident. The hoods of both cars spewed steam. The front door of the red Mustang was swung open and a young woman was dangling out, her head and arms inches from the pavement. The driver of the white Mirata

300

was slumped over the wheel. The horn blared.

Starr cursed. Caggiano looked back at Wolfe, who was watching the accident scene with widening eyes. "I'll call it in," said Caggiano. "See what you can do for them."

"What about—"

"He's cuffed and belted. Don't worry."

Wolfe began to howl, bouncing up and down on the seat.

Caggiano sneered at him. In an instant he slid over to the driver's seat and punched the car into gear. Tires squealed, and the smell of burning rubber filled the car.

"Hey!" Starr bellowed.

Caggiano looked in the mirror at Wolfe, who was now pinned to the back of the seat from the force of acceleration. He flipped a switch and the sirens and lights came alive. Cars and pedestrians scattered.

He looked again in the mirror. Wolfe's face registered terror.

"Scared, Wolfe?" Caggiano said. The siren's wail echoed off the buildings. The rolling lights reflected back into his eyes. "As scared as Damian Crystal was when you were beating her to death?"

Chapter 60

Barnett had his arm around Carol and Penny, and was taking them into his car when an officer rushed over.

"We just got a call from Starr. He and Caggiano were taking the suspect downtown." The officer had trouble catching his breath. "Caggiano took off."

"Took off?"

"With the suspect."

"In a cruiser?"

"Yes."

"Call Captain Wilson with the roof number. Have him dispatch Juneau." The officer ran to his car. "No radio. Use the phone." The man pivoted and dashed for the phone booth on the corner.

"What do you think John's doing?" Carol said in the car.

"I don't know, babe. My only concern is you and Penny."

"Mike, it's John. Something's terribly wrong. Go after him. Find him." She stopped. "Harlan didn't hurt us because Caggiano saved us."

"After I take you home."

When they reached their house, Penny was still

sobbing. Barnett carried her inside, placed her on the couch, and covered her with a quilt. He snuggled Felix into her chest. She clutched the stuffed toy.

"I'm okay, Mike. Really. Find John. He's your friend."

"I want Dr. Klein to come over. I'm calling him now."

His pager buzzed.

Barnett called Wilson who said the helicopter had spotted the car with roof number 440 at Hains Point.

"Let me handle this alone," Barnett warned. "This isn't like Caggiano. Something's fishy."

"I'm sending backup units. They'll stay clear until you summon them. We also have a lookout for Marybeth Wolfe."

Barnett rushed out the door. The two unmarked units he requested to stand guard had already arrived. "The alley in the rear," he said to one of them, then got into his car and sped off.

Marybeth Wolfe had just turned the corner when she saw the phalanx of police cars around her house. She smirked. Without missing a beat, she performed a U-turn and drove south on Vermont Avenue. By the White House, she made a right onto Pennsylvania and cruised to Connecticut Avenue where she made another left. She parked the car in an underground lot, walked outside, and hailed a cab.

National Airport was ten minutes away.

Chapter 61

Hains Point stuck out like a knife into the Potomac River cleaving the river from the Washington Channel. A one-way road wound around the perimeter. Parallel to the road, a bike and jogging trail was usually filled with fishermen trying for herring that fed on plants clinging to the footing of the concrete promenade. The interior held a small public golf course.

At the tip sat *The Awakening,* a massive steel statue of a man imbedded in soil. From above, it looked as if the earth was his blanket as the giant stretched and yawned with the new day. The only exposed areas were his face, right arm, left hand, half of his right foot and the bend of his left leg from thigh to shin.

Just across the river, the lights from National Airport's runway shone brightly. The random boom of cannons used to frighten birds mingled with the crackling sound of departing jets.

To the east, the thwaka-thwaka of military helicopters from Andrews Air Force Base ferrying VIPS to and from the Pentagon cut the air.

It was dusk and the park was officially closed.

Caggiano felt the wood mulch squish under his shoes as he dragged Wolfe out to the statue, throwing him into the giant's five-foot-high hand. The curved metal fingers made a canopy over Wolfe's head.

Still handcuffed, Wolfe had trouble getting his balance.

"They'll know it was you," he said, looking at Caggiano.

Caggiano stood solidly, his legs a body width apart. "Don't care." He stared at Wolfe. "What was she to you?"

"The hooker? Nothing. Just a whore."

With one large step, Caggiano was in front of Wolfe. He punched him in the stomach. Wolfe folded at the waist, the bottom of his spine hitting the hard statue, and he gasped.

"Why did you kill her?"

Wolfe struggled to stand erect and catch his breath. "Nothing. She was just a—"

Caggiano backhanded Wolfe's face, and the force slammed the killer's head against the giant's fingers. Wolfe's mouth bled. He sucked his lip, looked up at Caggiano.

"We used her . . . part of the therapy." Caggiano's brow furrowed as he listened. "I know what's wrong with me. Am I crazy because I want to get well?"

As Wolfe talked, Caggiano recalled Barnett telling him about Monika Sidor's assessment of the man based on the videotape. It was uncannily close.

"It's all in my scrapbook. At the house."

"Tell me about Damian."

Wolfe leaned back, the hand supporting his weight. "Okay," he said indignantly. "You want the short course, Psychology One-oh-one evaluation?"

With an air of detachment, he began. "He beat us.

He raped us both. By the time I was nine I could feel scar tissue in my anus. My sister suffered from chronic vaginal infections. We went to our mother, but she didn't believe us. 'He'd never do anything like that,' she said."

Caggiano rubbed his hand where he had hit Wolfe. It stung.

"I needed love. We both needed love. One day, when we were about ten or so, I read about sexual intercourse and how two people who love each other . . . We only had each other. We were the only ones we could trust and depend on. We used sex to protect ourselves from the hatred of the outside world, from our father, from everything."

Wolfe showed no emotion. Caggiano was taken by how clinical his speech was, how precise his words, how devoid of guilt he appeared. Wolfe picked up on Caggiano's contemptuous stare.

"I know what you think, but you don't understand. Nobody does. When we were together, nothing else mattered. I never felt so safe, secure in my life."

"Go on."

"One day," Wolfe's eyes became glassy, "Mother walked in on my sister and me. For the first time, we felt dirty. She made us feel dirty." He spat out the words. "She screamed and yelled at us. Father came running in and," Wolfe took a deep breath, "he beat us both in front of Mother. Then he yelled at Mother to leave so he could talk to us alone. It was then that he . . . I remember the look on my sister's face. . . . He made me watch."

Wolfe bobbed his head up and down. He lost his composure, slid down the palm to the dirt and cried.

Caggiano paced around the hand.

"I made up my mind then that he would never hurt us again." Wolfe stopped crying, burning his eyes into Caggiano. He stood.

"We devised a plan to poison him and blame it on Mother. When it came time to testify at the trial we were perfect." He spoke with pride. "We acted like little innocent children. Who would believe we were capable of such a thing?"

Caggiano saw a car about a mile away. He knew it was the police. "Damian, where did she fit in?"

"We were placed in a foster home until we were old enough to leave. Sister and I were still," he hesitated, "together. We loved each other—"

The headlights got brighter. "Damian!"

"Part of my therapy was to relive the experience of that night, the night Mother came in. I had to make it right, they said, through visualization. Make a different outcome, an outcome less traumatic. They said the past was past and I had to get beyond it. But I couldn't do it no matter how hard I tried. I had to have a live person, someone to actually act it out with. Damian was one of those persons. She didn't seem to mind if I got a little rough. She just charged me more money."

"Why did you have to kill her?"

"Something . . . I don't know . . . happened. It was an accident."

Caggiano hung his head. "I loved her. We were going to be—"

The car skidded on the grass. The high beams went on causing Caggiano to block his eyes with his hand.

"Mike, stay away," he screamed. Barnett froze. An elongated shadow of his body streaked across the turf.

"Cag. We can fix it. Whatever it is, we can fix it.

Let him go. We got him good and solid." He took a step closer.

"Stop. Don't come any farther." Caggiano pulled out his gun, aimed it at Wolfe.

"Cag, don't!"

He fired. A blue spark careened off one of the statue's fingers inches above Wolfe's head.

He folded to the ground.

Barnett gripped Caggiano's wrist and held it until he could pry the gun away.

"I loved her, Mike. I loved her . . ." Caggiano looked dazed. His eyes lifeless.

"Cag . . ."

Barnett looked over at Wolfe, who was curled up, fetal position, in the security of the huge hand.

Chapter 62

The police at Miami Airport scrutinized the arriving passengers on Delta flight #195 from Washington. A woman fitting Marybeth Wolfe's description, using her American Express card, had bought a ticket and, according to an employee, boarded the flight.

What the employee didn't know, however, was that a woman dressed in a cabin attendant's uniform walked off the plane moments before the gangway door closed, leaving behind her own clothes in the lavatory.

During the two hour, forty-five minute flight, Barnett had called the Dade County Sheriff's office three times to make certain Marybeth's arrival would be well attended. On the plane, a woman couldn't wait to land so she could tell her husband about her good fortune. While waiting in line, she received a free ticket from an airline representative as part of a special promotion.

When she was supposed to be in the air, Marybeth was on the ground, taking the Metro's yellow and red lines to Union Station. From there, a Metroliner transported her to Amtrak's Metropark station where she took a cab to Newark Airport.

In the gift shop, Marybeth purchased a small carry-on bag, some toiletries, Joseph Wambaugh's *The Blooding*, and a purple bikini.

She checked the TV monitor. Her flight to San Jose, Costa Rica, would be leaving in just under an hour.

Chapter 63

"What about the cereal?" Quill asked, holding a beer. He and Barnett were sitting in the living room.

"According to the medical reports in the scrapbook, their father sent them away frequently for mental health counseling. He did it to appease social workers who received complaints from their school teachers.

"The staff reported that whenever he would send them a package of their favorite foods, they would turn violent, even suicidal. He used those small breakfast cereal boxes as a trigger, to let them know he was still watching them, to show he still had control over them."

"Brainwashing."

"Exactly. Nobody at the hospital made the connection to cereal because they ate it every day. It was the small boxes that did it. You have to remember that that was more than twenty years ago. Mental health workers are a lot more aware of remote control techniques these days. Funny twist, too. Know how they killed their father? Poisoned his cereal."

Carol came into the room.

"And Cag?" he asked.

"When he got divorced he turned to prostitutes for companionship. He fell in love with Damian and wanted to marry her."

"It was a part of John's life that we never saw. He kept it hidden from everyone," said Carol.

"He considered it his personal failure," Barnett said. "He was ashamed."

Carol glanced at her husband.

Barnett caught her stare, held it for an instant, averted his eyes. He continued: "I think he really thought he loved her, and, you know, I think maybe she was a little fond of him . . . in a way."

"Then she was the leak," Quill said.

"Cag treated her like a wife. He told her about his day's work, what went on at the office. The usual. Only she told Wolfe. That's how he knew so much about our investigation. Early on, I don't think she knew that he was the killer. She probably suspected later but didn't say anything to Cag. She knew how jealous he was of her other clients."

Softly, Quill said, "How's Cag doing?"

"I saw him today. He's got a lot to sort out. It'll take time, but he's going to make it." Barnett hesitated. "The U.S. Attorney said he's got no plans to bring charges as long as Cag is under treatment."

"Do you think Cag really planned to kill Wolfe?"

"Yes, but when it came time to pull the trigger at Hains Point it just wasn't in him. He aimed high on purpose, thank God."

"And what about the sister, Marybeth?"

"We don't know where she is," said Barnett, shaking his head. "We thought we had her, but she snookered us."

"I knew them both. Can you believe it?" Carol said. "I keep replaying conversations that we had over the months." She shivered. "They seemed like normal people, just like you and me."

"Speak for yourself," Quill said.

Epilogue

Overlooking the Pacific Ocean at El Ocotal in Guanacaste province, the redhead in the purple bikini was reading a week-old copy of the *International Herald Tribune*. She took great interest in a feature story about the new science of "DNA Fingerprinting."

She crossed her legs, pulled down the brim of her floppy straw hat, and adjusted her sunglasses. She sipped a piña colada and looked down at waves crashing against the cliff above La Playa del Coco. From her perch in the terrace bar of the Hotel Ocotal, the black sand looked warm and sensual.

The story quoted District of Columbia Police Detective Mike Barnett who gleaned a DNA sample from skin cells left on an envelope sent by a serial killer. However, after authorities caught the killer, the sample didn't match.

"We think we know who the original sample came from, but we can't be sure until we find that person. High technology forensics does have its limits," the story quoted Barnett as saying.

She took another sip and studied the sky. It was azure blue and cloudless. A fishing boat cut across the water. A tamed bar parrot named Gabriella cooed in her ear.

She removed the story from the newspaper using her long sharp nails. She folded and placed it in the first page of a fresh scrapbook.

Marybeth Wolfe closed her eyes, listened to the surf and Gabriella. The soft breeze carried the smell of orchids.

She slept soundly.

Larry Kane, a pseudonym, is an investigative journalist and the author of six non-fiction books about crime and law enforcement. He has taught at police academies and seminars and is a consultant to law enforcement agencies on ritual crime and cult activities. He lives in Alexandria, VA, where he is also a licensed private investigator.

THE SEVENTH CARRIER SERIES
by Peter Albano

THE ONLY ALTERNATIVE IS ANNIHILATION . . .
RICHARD P. HENRICK

SILENT WARRIORS   (3026, $4.50)
The Red Star, Russia's newest, most technologically advanced
submarine, outclasses anything in the U.S. fleet. But when the
captain opens his sealed orders 24 hours early, he's staggered to
read that he's to spearhead a massive nuclear first strike against
the Americans!

THE PHOENIX ODYSSEY   (2858, $4.50)
All communications to the USS *Phoenix* suddenly and mysteri-
ously vanish. Even the urgent message from the president cancel-
ling the War Alert is not received and in six short hours the
Phoenix will unleash its nuclear arsenal against the Russian
mainland. . . .

COUNTERFORCE   (3025, $4.50)
In the silent deep, the chase is on to save a world from destruction. A single Russian submarine moves on a silent and sinister
course for American shores. The men aboard the U.S.S. *Triton*
must search for and destroy the Soviet killer submarine as an un-
suspecting world races for the apocalypse.

CRY OF THE DEEP   (3166, $4.50)
With the Supreme leader of the Soviet Union dead the Kremlin is
pointing a collective accusing finger towards the United States.
The motherland wants revenge and unless the USS *Swordfish* can
stop the Russian *Caspian,* the salvoes of World War Three are a
mere heartbeat away!

BENEATH THE SILENT SEA   (3167, $4.50)
The Red Dragon, Communist China's advanced ballistic missile-
carrying submarine embarks on the most sinister mission in human history: to attack the U.S. and Soviet Union simultaneously.
Soon, the Russian *Barkal,* with its planned attack on a single
U.S. submarine is about unwittingly to aid in the destruction of
all mankind!

*Available wherever paperbacks are sold, or order direct from the
Publisher. Send cover price plus 50¢ per copy for mailing and
handling to Zebra Books, Dept. 3513, 475 Park Avenue South,
New York, N.Y. 10016. Residents of New York, New Jersey and
Pennsylvania must include sales tax. DO NOT SEND CASH.*